STARSTRUCK

by

Kevin O'Hagan

Grosvenor House
Publishing Limited

This book is published by
Grosvenor House Publishing Ltd
Link House
140 The Broadway, Tolworth, Surrey, KT6 7HT.
www.grosvenorhousepublishing.co.uk

This book is a work of fiction. Any resemblance to
people or events, past or present, is purely coincidental.

A CIP record for this book
is available from the British Library

ISBN 978-1-83615-129-6

Other Books by the Author

Battlescars
No Hiding Place
Last Stand
Killing Time
A Change of Heart
Blood Tracks
The Key to Murder
Murder in Store
Buried Secrets
Avenging Angel

In memory of my good friend Tony

A gentleman, scholar and warrior

Acknowledgements

As always, my huge thanks to the 'Usual Suspects', who helped me on my journey from getting this story from an idea to print.

My daughter Lauren for the proofreading, grammar and spellcheck.

My son Tom for yet another excellent cover design.

My publishers for all their help and guidance, especially Melanie Bartle.

My wife Tina for her continued support of my writing and the tea, coffee and occasional Jack Daniel's on the rocks.

Special thanks to all the music greats, alive and dead, that have enriched my life since I was a young boy and influenced this story.

Author's Note

Some places and locations in this novel exist in real life; others are purely fictional, as may be their geographical placings. Landscapes, names and layouts take on another imaginary status in this book.

All the characters are purely fictional, as are their stories.

Thank you for indulging me to help in creating this story.

A Word from the Author

After writing *Blood Tracks* in 2022, I thought about the possibility of bringing back the only survivor of the book: Ricky Wilder.

But how? Where would he be? What would he be doing a few years on from the horrific murders on Ruma Island?

Then, I had an inkling of an idea that could possibly work to give him another storyline.

This book is set in Las Vegas, Nevada. It is a place I know well and have visited many times.

You either love Vegas or you hate it.

I love it.

I love its past, its history and its present.

It is a magical place.

Las Vegas does what it says on the tin. It entertains.

Las Vegas is pure escapism, where anything truly goes.

So, I thought about Ricky having a residency playing at a hotel and casino.

It is a final swansong to one of the greatest rock 'n' roll frontmen ever.

A record company want him to record his live show, as does a film company.

He is suddenly the Renaissance man.

Ricky is also planning to get married.

Things are finally looking settled for him, but there is a cloud on the horizon.

A dangerous stalker is after him.

Now, it is time to have some fun and games, filled with unexpected twists and turns as we follow the character's journey, indulging my passion of music along the way.

Enjoy!

Kevin O'Hagan, September 2024

The first ever single I bought was 'Starman' by David Bowie (1972) and my first live concert was Mott the Hoople in 1973/4. This started my lifelong passion for music.

"The lady's starstruck, she's nothing but bad luck,
the lady's starstruck running after me"

Rainbow
From the album *Rainbow Rising*

"Girls will be boys and boys will be girls
It's a mixed up, muddled up, shook up world"

The Kinks, 'Lola'

Prologue

Ruma Island, Outer Hebrides, 2024

"Here we are, ladies and gentlemen. Welcome to Ruma Island. If you would please tread carefully when you disembark the boat. Once we're all off, we will then begin our tour."

Tour guide Anna Murray paused to let the assembled group of 20 alight the boat and step foot on the barren and rugged landscape of the island.

A watery sun hung in the grey sky and dark rainclouds threatened. After all, it was summer, and for the people who lived in this remote part of the UK, the current weather was pretty fair.

Once they were all on dry land, Anna instructed the group to follow her. She told them that it was fine to take photographs of the island and the outside of the house they would visit, but photography inside the house was strictly forbidden.

Their first stop on the tour was a brass plaque on a small granite stone near the dock. It was a memorial to all who had lost their lives in the murderous slaughter that took place here on 20 October 2022.

It was a poignant moment for the assembled group. There was a mix of British, French, Germany, Chinese and American tourists.

After five minutes or so, Anna led them on.

"Please watch your footing on the ground. It can be uneven in places. And if you see any cats, please don't attempt to pet them as they are wild and indigenous to the island."

"What species are they?" asked a middle-aged British man.

"They are called *sorees*. They're like a small bobcat to look at," replied Anna. "Nobody really knows how they came to live on the island. It's one of Ruma's many mysteries."

The group walked on. Then, after ten minutes or so, a magnificent gothic building appeared before them.

"Ladies and gentlemen, let me introduce you to the murder house itself: *An Diadan*. This is the scene of what has been dubbed by the press as the 'Ruma Island Slaughterhouse'."

Anna paused to let the group take in the magnificent façade of the Gothic house.

A German voice from the group asked what *An Diadan* meant. Anna told them that it meant 'haven' or 'retreat'.

She loved this first part of the tour the most, as it allowed her to study the expressions on people's faces when they realised that they were actually looking at the very house where the legendary rock band Stormtrooper and their recording crew had met a tragic fate during a night of terror and bloodshed unlike anything seen in the British Isles.

One member of the band did survive. Lead singer Ricky Wilder. Badly injured and mentally traumatised, he managed to escape the island.

The story had dominated the front pages of the press for weeks and has since become a fixture on many true crime channels and the subject of numerous books and internet articles.

The house had gained the same notoriety as the Amityville House on Long Island, New York – the scene of murder, possession and hauntings that became world famous in the 1970s and 1980s.

After his escape from *An Diadan*, Wilder had become a sought-after figure among just about every media outlet eager for interviews about the events of that fateful night. These days, he was in demand more for his harrowing experience on the island than for his music career.

After he had spent some months in rehab, Ricky was well enough to tell the tale.

The band had come to Ruma to record a comeback album after many years apart. The isolated island and house, which had then belonged to legendary film director Harvey Barnes, had a state-of-the-art underground recording studio, where many famous music stars had previously recorded.

It seemed a perfect place to cut the band's new record.

How wrong they had been.

The history of the band had been well documented. The original line-up had the charismatic but unpredictable Jimmy Parrish as their lead singer. Parrish was a great frontman, but a loose cannon who became increasingly unreliable due to his struggles with alcohol and cocaine addiction.

One fateful night, during a drug-fuelled party to celebrate his 26th birthday aboard Parrish's yacht,

Seawolf, tragedy struck. Jimmy reportedly fell overboard and drowned, but his body was never recovered.

The band continued with lead guitarist Ricky Wilder taking over the reins as frontman.

The success of the Mark II line up grew and grew. They became bigger than the original, although there was always suspicion hanging over them about Jimmy Parrish's death.

There had been much infighting and animosity within the band at that time, leading some to believe that tensions could have escalated to the point of murder.

Nothing was ever proven and the band split in 2000 after huge global success.

That said, they continued to have a huge fanbase. The interest in the band never died.

When arriving on the island, the unsuspecting band didn't realise the woman who was there to oversee their stay was, in fact, Parrish's adopted daughter, Sydney Rose, who believed the band were responsible for her father's death.

Along with her stepbrother Noah, they had meticulously planned their revenge.

When the island was cut off by a raging storm, they began their bloody slaughter of all the assembled group.

In their twisted and deluded minds, they were doing the right thing and were hell bent on finishing Stormtrooper forever and gaining justice for Jimmy Parrish.

But Ricky Wilder had more resolve than the other victims and fought back and killed them both before making his escape.

* * *

Anna now dramatically held up a large brass set of keys in her hand.

"Now, are we all ready to enter the house and see exactly where the murders occurred?"

A murmur of anticipation ran through the assembled group.

"Don't worry, there are no ghosts lurking inside as far as I know, but we do like to be careful. That's why we hold ours tours in daylight hours. Just in case."

While this was partially true, the island was also incredibly remote, making it difficult and dangerous to navigate even in daylight, let alone at night.

Tours in the wee small hours were not an option.

Anna walked up the steps, past the imposing ornate stone statues of two evil looking devil dogs, inserted the key in the lock and turned it.

The door swung open.

"Could you wait one second while I switch on the lights?"

Anna disappeared inside as the group waited.

Suddenly, there was an unearthly scream from inside.

Everybody froze and looked at each other.

The door then burst open wide, revealing a hooded figure in black brandishing a knife.

The crowd pulled back in horror between screams and startled intakes of breath.

Then, the figure reached up and pulled down the hood, revealing a young smiling face.

"Hello, everybody. My name is Adam and I'll be assisting Anna with the tour today."

The group laughed nervously, quickly regaining their composure as they realised it wasn't a gruesome apparition returned from the grave to seek vengeance.

Adam Burns ran his hand through his unruly blonde hair and then stood to one side and gestured with his hand.

"Apologies if I scared some of you, but that's the nature of this tour, which I'm sure you are all well aware of. Please come inside as we reveal the building's grisly secrets. Welcome once again to *An Diadan*. I urge you all to stay together and don't wander off on your own, for your own safety."

The group slowly entered the house, wondering what other surprises were in store for them.

* * *

In the wake of the murders, the island's owner had sold up. Harvey Barnes was a reclusive millionaire who had used the island and house as a sanctuary in the summer months for many years, but now he was deeply shocked by what had occurred at his home and said that he could never return.

The house remained boarded up for some time, and boats were no longer permitted to sail to Ruma Island.

A year later, a large Asian entertainment group announced their intention to buy the island and launch what they dubbed 'Murder Tours'.

Interest in the so-called Ruma Island Slaughterhouse murders remained strong worldwide, presenting a lucrative opportunity for the group to cash in on the avid followers of true crime and fans of Stormtrooper, who could treat the island as a site of pilgrimage.

Within six months, the operation was up and running, and the money began to pour in as customers started arriving.

The experience wasn't cheap; you had to fly to mainland Scotland, then take another flight to the Outer Hebrides, landing at the small airport of Benbecula. From there, guests had to board a boat for a choppy hour-long ride to the island before the tour could begin.

In some circles, the whole thing was seen as distasteful, while for others, it represented a place of intrigue and myth.

Murder held a grisly fascination for many members of the public.

The Ruma Island slaughter was up there with Jack the Ripper and Ted Bundy when it came to continued fascination and interest in serial killers.

* * *

The group was now taken on a guided tour of the house, visiting each room in the order where the murders had occurred.

Everything had been recreated as it had been back on that fateful night. The only things missing were the bodies.

The swimming pool was still there where the bodies of the young co-engineers, Kerry Piper and Jude Green, were found.

The hot tub where the band's bassist, Rory Doyle, was murdered.

The American bar where drummer, Ray Hawkins, met his demise.

The group visited the recording studio deep in the bowels of the house where the band's authentic instruments were still housed, along with scribbled lyrics in notepads.

Fans of Stormtrooper stared in awe at the last place the band had ever recorded.

The album *In the Dying Light* had gone on posthumously to top the charts around the world and was the band's bestselling release.

Every part of the house was open for investigation, including the island with the circle of Callanish standing stones where Ricky Wilder had hidden out, as well as the maintenance shed where he ultimately killed Noah Rose, aka Kenny Holton.

Also, the legendary 'Mission Control' study, where Sidney Rose had cameras on every area of the house, allowing her to monitor everyone's movements on that fateful night and track their whereabouts. This is where she had carefully orchestrated her warped plans along with her stepbrother.

Macabre as it may have seemed to impartial members of the public, for fans, it was a voyeur's paradise filled with memorabilia, facts, myths and legends.

The group were now all standing on the upper landing where each member of the recording crew had slept.

As Adam Burns continued his tour spiel, an attractive red-headed woman in her late 30s raised her hand from the assembled gathering and asked, "Excuse me, which room did Ricky sleep in, and can we see it?"

Her voice held an American accent.

Adam smiled.

"Yes, we will see it and we'll get to it soon. It's on the second floor, along with the rooms of all the band members. Ricky's room was number 6, but first, we'll check out rooms 1 to 5."

With that, he entered room number 1, and the group followed, all except the red-headed woman, who lingered behind. Once they had disappeared inside, she quietly made her way down the corridor to the staircase, ascending to the second floor and heading straight for room number 6.

The door was unlocked.

She entered it and stood mesmerised at the surroundings.

A shiver ran through her body.

She had waited so long to get a ticket for this tour. They were like gold dust, but finally, she had made it here.

She surveyed the surroundings.

Yes, the room was luxurious, but that was not the reason she stood in awe.

It was because the legendary Ricky Wilder had stayed here.

He had slept in that bed and showered in that bathroom.

She walked around the room looking for any tangible evidence left of the man.

She opened the wardrobe and all the drawers, finding them completely empty.

She breathed in the air and touched every surface.

Then, the woman entered the bathroom, slipped off her shoes and stood in the shower cubicle, imagining Ricky standing there naked soaping his body.

For a man in his mid-60s, he was still in great shape.

A true, living, breathing rock god.

A member of a very small surviving group.

Bands of today could not hold a torch to the Ricky Wilders of the past.

He was a dying breed.

Along with the likes of Robert Plant, Ian Gillan, David Coverdale, Brian Johnson and Ozzy Osbourne, to name but a few. The music world would never witness such rock royalty ever again. Men with true charisma who could have an audience eating out the palm of their hands.

The woman now visualised Wilder towelling down his taunt body in front of the large ornate mirror on the wall.

Leaving the bathroom, she headed to the king-size bed.

Lying on the bed, she hugged and sniffed the pillow, fantasising he was next to her ready to make love.

What she would give for this.

But Ricky Wilder had got himself a new girlfriend and rumours of marriage were circulating in the press.

What could this woman give him?

It was another mistake. But Ricky was always unlucky in love.

He needed somebody who really understood him. Somebody who would look after his every need. He needed true love, not some whim.

She then heard voices and footsteps below as the group came out of room 1 into the corridor.

Silently opening the bedroom door, she heard the voice of Adam saying, "We are now entering the bedroom of the producer Brody Willis."

She waited until they had gone in and allowed herself another private look at the room.

Was it her imagination or was there a faint smell of Hugo Boss? Ricky's favourite aftershave.

The woman silently left the room, but not before taking a dozen or more photos and recording a video on her phone.

She retraced her footsteps to rejoin the group, unnoticed by anybody.

What an exciting moment it had been to spend time alone in the room of her idol.

She wasn't really interested in the tour itself; she just wanted to experience what Ricky had.

This trip had been a long time coming, but it had been worth every penny and every mile to get here.

She had followed Stormtrooper, and particularly Ricky, ever since she had been in her early 20s.

She hadn't been a great fan of the music scene at that time. R&B and rap wasn't for her.

Growing up, she had heard some classic 80s Stormtrooper singles on the radio but didn't know much more until her uncle introduced her to his collection of the band's albums. And that was all it took to sell her on their music.

Then came the DVDs of the band's live performances, and that's when she saw Ricky Wilder in action, completely mesmerised by him. She fell in love there and then.

No other man could compete.

Today's men weren't real men anyway.

They didn't know who they were and what they were supposed to be.

They had been emasculated to within an inch of their lives.

Finally, when Stormtrooper had reformed a few years ago for the charity concert *British Metal Legends*

Battle COVID, she had the chance to see her idol live, and it exceeded all her expectations and more.

The woman hadn't been old enough to see the band the first time around, but it didn't matter. Finally, she got her wish.

She knew everything about Ricky Wilder.

In fact, she was his biggest fan.

She loved him unconditionally.

She would do anything for her idol. Absolutely anything.

There was a rumour in the entertainment world that Ricky was going to make a solo comeback in Las Vegas with a residency there.

How exciting. She lived and worked in Las Vegas.

What a stroke of luck.

Ricky was hers and she would have him at any costs.

One way or another, they would be together forever.

Chapter 1

Las Vegas, two weeks later

It's midnight and Ricky Wilder is enjoying a Jack Daniel's on the rocks, seated in the plush surroundings of the Chameleon Lounge at the Sunset Hotel and Casino in Las Vegas.

The hotel was located east of the famous Strip, nestled between Paradise Road and East Flamingo Road. It was just a block away from the now-defunct Hard Rock Hotel and Casino, which had since become Virgin Hotels Las Vegas.

Ricky was just a week away from the end of his first residency playing at the Sunset. He was here from the start of May to the end of September. The residency had been a total success, selling out every night.

The concert theatre, known as the Midnight Auditorium, had hosted many big names over the years and now it was Ricky Wilder's turn – the legendary former frontman of Stormtrooper and later Wilder Things.

A man who had truly embraced the rockstar life and a man also known for being the sole survivor of the Ruma Island slaughter.

A man scarred physically and mentally, but fighting his way back into the spotlight.

Ricky was playing a solo acoustic set here. The show was called 'Stripped Back'.

The set featured a mix of his solo songs, tracks from Wilder Things – his later, short-lived band – and some classic Stormtrooper hits.

Stormtrooper had toured America a few times during their heyday but had never played in Las Vegas itself, despite visiting on several occasions for some wild days of R&R between concert dates.

Las Vegas truly was the centre of celebrity, glitz and glamour.

Ricky loved the place. That's why he didn't hesitate when he was offered the residency.

He was getting back to his old self and his confidence was gradually returning.

Many tough months of therapy were behind him. He hoped he was finally on the mend.

This "Stripped Back" set was something new for both him and the fans, but he was relishing the simplicity of just the guitar, piano and himself on stage.

The audience, respectful of Ricky's long and distinguished career in the rock world, was receptive to all his music, but they ultimately looked forward to the Stormtrooper tracks, particularly the classic 'Tough Love' and the arena favourite 'You Are My Shot in the Arm'.

Before coming out to Las Vegas, Ricky had received an MBE for his contribution to the music world. It had been a total shock to him, but something he truly treasured.

He had done many diverse and interesting things in his life, but travelling up to Buckingham Palace and receiving his medal from HRH Prince William was a proud and exciting moment.

His only regret was that his old bandmates weren't there to witness and share it with him.

After the demise of the other members of Stormtrooper, the band were posthumously entered into the Rock 'n' Roll Hall of Fame for a second time, joining a very exclusive club.

That had been a great achievement and honour, but the MBE was the icing on the cake in a long career that could have ended that night on Ruma Island.

With the help of a few good psychiatrists, Ricky was pretty much coming to terms with what had happened on that fateful night. He would always miss his bandmates and friends, but he had somehow managed to rebuild his career and life to begin writing a new chapter.

At 66 years of age, the days of long tours and arena concerts were behind him.

He fleetingly toyed with the idea of Stormtrooper Mark III, but quickly dismissed it. His heart wasn't really in it. Plus, he didn't think he had the resolve or energy for it any longer even if he was up for the idea.

Although he was still in shape, running around on stage for 2.5 hours every night was now a big ask.

Sometimes he missed it, especially after catching the Rolling Stones on their latest tour, where Jagger, the old bastard, was still shaking those hips at 80. Then there was Bruce Springsteen, now in his early 70s, still putting on three-hour-plus gigs.

Ricky rationalised that Jagger hadn't been shot in the leg or hacked about with a machete, nor had he fought for his life as Ricky had.

Also, Ricky couldn't see himself living off carrot juice and hummus. He was never going to be a vegan.

He enjoyed a steak or pulled pork sandwich far too much.

He was a child of the 60s and 70s. A time where you couldn't afford to be fussy with what you ate.

The big arenas had also eroded Ricky's voice somewhat, and while it still retained a rich, gritty quality, some of the high notes were now beyond his reach.

Stormtrooper had come in the wake of a second wave of heavy rock bands, such as Iron Maiden, Saxon, Van Halen, Judas Priest, Motley Crue and AC/DC.

They had been wild times of booze, drugs, women and song.

That was what rockstars – and their fans – did back then.

It was expected and part of the deal.

The more controversy that surrounded you, the better your record sold.

Drugs was a massive part of the lifestyle.

Ricky recalled a time when Stormtrooper played a massive sell out open-air summer gig at the stately home of Brackenfield Hall in Surrey.

Weeks before the event, drug dealers were out in the fields beyond the hall burying drugs and contraband ready to dig up and sell on the day of the concert to fans. That was how crazy it had been.

Ricky had long given up the stereotypical rockstar life.

The residency here with the acoustic set was just nice for him.

He had an affinity with the States, especially Vegas.

He had married his first wife, the pornstar Tracey Ann Gold, here in the famous Little White Chapel.

Ricky had lived in Florida for a while until the marriage broke up. Then, he returned to Great Britain.

He had recently bumped into Tracey in Las Vegas. She was there with her daughter from her second marriage and three grandchildren, on a coach tour of the Golden West, having stopped in Vegas for a few days.

The voluptuous, sexy woman he once knew, celebrated for her roles in such Hollywood epics as *Up All Night* and *Gangbang 1 & 2*, had gracefully transitioned into a slightly plump middle-aged grandma.

How times had changed. He wondered if her daughter knew about her past.

His second marriage to weathergirl, Louise Scott, had also failed and she had left him in one of the many squally showers they experienced together.

He had lost track of Louise, but he did know she was no longer doing television work. He heard some time ago that she was now a successful author of children's books.

Ricky had been an infamous womaniser in his earlier days. Being in a world successful rock band meant there had been no shortage of female admirers.

Though he knew he could never be faithful to just one woman, he had always been a hopeless romantic at heart.

But as the old saying goes, "You can't have your cake and eat it."

Those days were now well and truly behind him too.

He was in a serious relationship. Ricky was dating rising TV star, Abigail Frost, and he was in love. She was the star of the long running US police series *New York Blue*, where she played Sergeant Nancy Quinn of the NYPD.

Abagail had been born in Cambridge in the UK, but had immigrated with her family to Boston, Massachusetts when she was 14 years old.

She had been an Olympic-level swimmer, winning a bronze medal in the 200m breaststroke in Athens in 2004. After a successful career in the pool, she transitioned into coaching in her early 30s. Upon retiring, she ventured into television, starting with commercials and then moving on to game and quiz shows. From there, her opportunities expanded, and her star began to shine brightly.

For a number of years, she had been married to baseball player Bradley Judd. Judd was a successful player until a back injury curtailed a promising career. This devastated him, and he hit the bottle hard, eventually becoming an alcoholic.

Alcohol changed his personality and, when drunk, he physically abused Abigail. Eventually, she divorced him.

Judd tragically died of alcohol poisoning at the age of 36.

In the years that followed, Abigail dated a few men, but found nobody serious until she met Ricky.

Of course, she knew who he was; he was world famous. But when she met him, he was down to earth and grounded, nothing like the man in the wild rock 'n' roll stories she had heard.

Ricky had dabbled in acting, notably playing the role of Marty Isles, a corrupt nightclub owner and drug trafficker, in the Netflix series *Above the Law*.

He first met Abigail in a crossover episode of both their shows.

They hit it off immediately and although she was 20 years younger than Ricky, they seemed made for each other.

Both were apart due to work commitments at the time, but six months later, they bumped into each other at an awards ceremony and their relationship blossomed.

Abigail had helped Ricky get back on his feet.

They had been together for nearly a year, and rumours were swirling that marriage was on the cards.

For the first time in a long while, Ricky was feeling happy.

* * *

Sitting with Ricky was his current manager, Joey Bruce. Joey had been managing him for a couple of years since Ricky formed the band Wilder Things after his time with Stormtrooper.

He was a no-nonsense Scot from Glasgow. Fifty years of age, single and married to the music industry.

Joey had managed some big stars in his time and had also been in a new wave band himself in the 80s. He knew his way around the business and looked after Ricky's interests.

On Ricky's part, he never imagined he would find a replacement for his old friend and manager, Bernie Garvey – God bless his soul. However, Joey had proven to be a true godsend.

Sitting on a barstool and surveying the room was Cecil Coombs, Ricky's minder in the US. A muscular Black man, he weighed a formidable 127 kilos and stood 6 feet 7 inches tall, making him an imposing presence and an effective deterrent against overzealous fans.

Cecil was from New York and had been a linebacker back in the day for the Giants. A knee injury put pay to his career prematurely. But now he was making good money as a bodyguard to the rich and famous.

Cecil sipped his mineral water and casually scrolled his phone, but his attention was firmly on the room.

Ricky drained his glass, signalled to the bartender and then looked at Joey Bruce.

"Another, Joey?"

Joey shook his head.

"Better not. I need to keep a clear head. I'm heading down to the casino soon. I have a game of poker waiting for me. Why not join me? It's in a private room."

"No thanks, Joey. Gambling and me don't go. I'm gonna give Abi a ring. She's working in London and should be available as it's early afternoon there in the UK. Then I'll turn in."

Joey smiled.

"You're getting old, Ricky."

Ricky laughed.

"Not old, just older."

Joey also laughed.

"Good title for a song, my friend."

Ricky shook his head.

"Bon Jovi beat me to it, I believe. A track on their *Crush* album in 2000."

A waiter brought Ricky's drink over, placing it on a coaster before picking up his empty glass. Ricky lifted his fresh drink and took a sip.

Joey got to his feet.

"Right, I'll love you and leave you. Maybe I'll see you for breakfast, if not rehearsals at 11.00am."

Ricky raised his glass.

"Best of luck on the tables."

Ricky watched as Joey Bruce left the room just as Gabriel Hart, the hotel's entertainment manager, entered the lounge.

He was in his late 30s. Tall and Slim. His short blonde hair was styled in a GI buzz cut. He had impossibly flawless white teeth.

For a man who lived in one of the hottest cities in the world, his skin was deathly pale. He was not a fan of sunbathing and obsessed over catching skin cancer.

His face didn't have a line on it, partly down to a healthy lifestyle and partly down to Botox.

He was magnificently camp and unashamedly bisexual. He was the epitome of Sin City itself.

Ricky had to admit that he was a strikingly handsome man.

Gabriel spotted Ricky and headed in his direction.

He sported a purple designer suit and jangled as he walked due to the copious amounts of jewellery he was wearing. He looked for all the world like a shop window mannequin from *Bloomingdale's* come to life.

"Ricky, darling. What a set. The crowd absolutely loved it. The place is a sellout again tomorrow night. Fucking magic. You have the Midas touch."

Gabriel was in charge of running the Midnight Auditorium and looked after all the acts that played there.

Back in the day, Las Vegas was often seen as a singer's graveyard, a place where legends like Elvis Presley and Frank Sinatra spent their later years as their popularity began to wane.

But now Vegas was a hot ticket for all the big acts.

Sir Rod Stewart was just finishing up a 13-year residency at Caesar's Palace on the Strip.

Donny and Marie Osmond had clocked up an incredible 1,730 shows at the Flamingo.

Sir Elton John had just completed his 469th and final concert at the Allegiant Stadium.

Famous names from the past, like Liberace and the Rat Pack, through to Barry Manilow, Cher, Sir Tom Jones, Celine Dion, and more recently, Lady Gaga and Adele, all graced the stages of Sin City.

Las Vegas was still the entertainment capital of the world. It was constantly evolving, never sitting back on its past glories or reputation.

Just down the road from the Sunset Hotel was the awe-inspiring MSG Sphere, which opened in 2023. Originally scheduled to debut in 2021, its opening was delayed due to COVID. The sphere stands an impressive 388ft tall and can seat between 17,500 and 20,000 people. U2 was the first act to perform there, launching their *Achtung Baby* tour in 2023 to tremendous success.

Las Vegas was thriving, its image transformed from that of the mafia and gangsters to one of successful entrepreneurs. These visionaries were building new, larger, and cutting-edge hotels, concert arenas and sports complexes all along and beyond the Strip.

The Sunset Hotel and Casino was only three years old and had been built on the site of the old Three Aces. The hotel was spread over 18.7 acres and boasted 670 rooms and 86 suites.

For a hotel off the Strip, it was hugely successful and always busy all year around.

Gabriel loved his job.

He had previously worked in downtown Fremont Street at the famous Golden Nugget, which first opened in 1946. Gabriel started as a bartender while also pursuing his passion for singing part-time. Over the course of ten years in Las Vegas, he worked his way up the ranks, progressing from receptionist to concierge, then party planner and finally to entertainment manager.

He had seen all that Vegas had to offer from the good to the mad to the bad.

Gabriel loved the entertainment world, especially music acts.

Born in Iowa, a Midwestern US state nestled between the Missouri and Mississippi rivers, Gabriel hailed from a region known for its rolling plains and expansive cornfield. Not exactly the cutting-edge capital of the world.

His parents owned a farm and were hard-working, god-fearing people.

Childhood was not a great time for Gabriel, who grew up as an only child. His parents' staunch religious beliefs, viewing any pleasures of the flesh outside of marriage as a mortal sin, created significant turmoil for young Gabriel as he struggled with his own sexuality. With no one to confide in, he lived in constant fear of the terrible consequences he believed would befall him if he offended God.

His only escape from feelings of guilt and moral confusion was his love of music. The music in this area was mainly country, gospel or bluegrass, but he had an uncle, Thomas, who had played in a band when he was younger and had lived in LA for a while.

Thomas had a passion for rock 'n' roll and introduced it to a young Gabriel, who instantly fell in love with the music. Gabriel spent hours at his uncle's house listening to his extensive collection of vinyl.

Then, Gabriel got into Guns n' Roses, Bon Jovi, Motley Crue, Iron Maiden, Van Halen and, of course, Stormtrooper.

Gabriel realised eventually that he was bisexual. He fancied Madonna like crazy, but also had a crush on George Micheal.

Growing up in Iowa was no picnic for him. He had to hide his true sexuality and urges from his parents, schoolfriends and neighbours. Homosexuality was not declared legal within the whole of the US until 2003.

Come 21 years of age, he was ready to leave the Midwest and head to LA to seek his fortune and finally be himself.

He longed to be a performer. He loved to sing.

His parents tried everything to keep him in Iowa, but he was determined to break free and live his own life away from the stifling suffocation of home.

One day, he just packed a suitcase and left while his parents were working. He never saw them again. He didn't need them or their bigoted views.

Whether they were now dead or alive, Gabriel had no idea and he didn't care.

He moved to LA and immersed himself in the vibrant Westside gay scene, finding sanctuary and a sense of belonging in clubs like Catch One. Gabriel rubbed shoulders with many celebrities and stars exploring their own sexuality, even spotting Freddie Mercury, frontman of Queen, there on multiple occasions.

He worked as a bartender and waiter in various bars and clubs, earning a decent living while trying to leave his past and Iowa roots behind.

Although he loved LA, his heart was set on living in Las Vegas. He remembered watching a programme about the city as a teenager and he fell instantly in love with its glitzy glamour and its melting pot of people from all walks of life.

When he finally came to Vegas and worked at the Golden Nugget, he occasionally sang and danced in a group called the Transformers.

He was a decent enough singer, but soon realised he wasn't destined to set the world on fire. Instead, he decided to look after the stars rather than become one himself, transitioning to the other side of the entertainment industry.

He still occasionally kept his hand in with a bit of singing and dancing when he could find time, but he mainly loved to work the entertainment scene.

So, ten years along the road with much travelling and experience under his belt, he had arrived in Vegas and he knew that this was the place he wanted to be.

Anything goes here and you can be whoever you want to be.

Gabriel enjoyed the freedom and the lack of judgement.

Viva Las Vegas.

* * *

"Glad you liked the show, Gabriel. Do you fancy a drink?" said Ricky.

"I shouldn't really, but you, Ricky, bring the wild side out in me, no pun intended."

Ricky signalled to the bartender again and immediately a waiter appeared at the table.

"What's your poison, Gabriel?"

"Pink gin and tonic please, Vincent. I'm in a decadent mood tonight."

The waiter disappeared and returned within minutes with the drink.

"So, how was your recent holiday to the UK?" asked Ricky.

"Absolutely delightful. The British are so helpful and polite. I had a wonderful time. I didn't want to come back."

"Where did you visit when you were over there?"

"Oh, you know, all the landmarks in and around London and a few other places. I even visited Lewisham where you were born."

"How did you know I was born there?" queried Ricky.

Gabriel rolled his eyes.

"Come on, Ricky, love, if I'm to look after you for five months of the year, I'm going to do my research, aren't I?"

He sipped his gin thoughtfully.

"So, is it true that you're getting married again?"

"I see the old rumour mill is turning."

"You know what social media is like. It likes its pound of flesh. Ricky, sweetheart, even in your – how shall I put it – advancing years, you're still one of the most eligible bachelors on the planet. Please tell me it isn't true that you're tying the knot! I've already missed my chance with George Clooney! Thousands of females and probably a few males will be gutted if you say it's so."

Ricky laughed.

"My lips are sealed for now."

"Well, fuck you then," said Gabriel grinning, "I bet if I contacted *Hello* magazine, they would already have your wedding pencilled in."

Ricky finished his drink.

"You're such a moody bitch."

"Damn right I am, darling."

Ricky stood up.

"Any way, time for bed."

Gabriel eyed him coyly.

"Is that an offer?"

"I'm sure you're not short on admirers, Gabriel."

"True. But I need to find one I like."

Ricky signalled to Cecil.

"Goodnight, Gabriel."

Cecil joined Ricky and Gabriel appraised him.

"I suppose you wouldn't like to buy me another drink and keep me company, big fellow?"

Cecil looked down at him.

"I'm still on duty."

Gabriel watched Ricky and Cecil leave.

He decided he might venture out into the night life.

He couldn't bear the thought of his empty suite on the fourth floor, with a television boasting 57 channels and nothing on – just like Bruce Springsteen had once sung about.

He fancied dancing and maybe having some meaningless sex. Time to get the glad rags on.

Chapter 2

Cecil walked Ricky to his suite on the top floor and bid him goodnight.

He waited until his boss was safely inside and then strolled down the corridor to his room four doors away.

Once inside his suite, Ricky took off his jacket and kicked off his shoes. He took out his phone and pressed Abigail's number. She answered on the second ring.

"Hello, Mr Rockstar. How did the show go?"

"Hi, baby. It all went well. I was pleased with it," replied Ricky, "So was the management. There's already talk of the residency next year."

"That's great news, Ricky. I'm so pleased it's going well. How are you in yourself?"

Ricky had taken a break from performing after experiencing a mini breakdown, despite his progress in recovery. For a time, he lost his confidence and struggled with stage fright.

Doctors explained that it was all tied to the trauma he experienced on Ruma Island and the loss of his band and team. They told him that there was no rhyme or reason to when these feelings would manifest themselves. It was something he would have to learn to live with.

For a while, it looked like Ricky might never perform again, but then his manager, Joey Bruce, had contacted him about the possibility of doing this residency.

No band. No sideshow. Just him. A solo acoustic set.

Ricky Wilder was huge in America and still a name that sold tickets. The idea appealed to him and, slowly but surely, he made his comeback.

"I'm doing fine, Abi. I have the odd wobble now and again, but apart from that, I'm on top of things. The management team are first class and look after me well."

"I'm glad to hear that. I worry about you, darling," replied Abigail.

"I know you do, sweetheart, but I'm fine. Anyway, enough about me. What about you? What are your plans for this afternoon?"

Abi excitedly told him.

'We're shooting some scenes in Trafalgar Square. These episodes shot here in London are going to be really good for the show. They'll feature in next season's opening episodes."

"That's great news. Do you know when you'll be home?"

"Hopefully, by the end of the week. I plan to be in Vegas on Friday, all being well."

"That's great news, honey. I'm missing you big time," said Ricky.

"Is that right? Well, I've just stepped out the shower, so maybe I'll send you a little photo to remind you of what you're missing," replied Abi.

"I can't wait."

"Oh shit, sorry. Room service is at the door with my lunch. I have to go. Love you."

"Love you too. Have a great afternoon and don't forget the pic."

Ricky's phone went dead.

He smiled to himself as he undressed and hit the shower.

The shower stall was as big as a small bedroom, complemented by a separate marble deep soaking tub in his suite. The room also featured its own bar and a lounge area with a 42-inch plasma screen television and DVD player. Floor-to-ceiling windows offered an excellent view of the city.

Vegas knew how to do things in style.

Stormtrooper first came here in 1981. They were filming a video for their then latest single 'Roll of the Dice'. The song had nothing to do with gambling, but the name of the record got them a visit to Sin City.

They stayed in the now demolished Stardust Hotel. An iconic symbol of the golden days of Vegas.

In between filming, they saw the legendary illusionists, Siegfried and Roy, perform there and they also went to Caesar's Palace to watch Sugar Ray Leonard take on Thomas 'The Hitman' Hearns on 18 September in the boxing match of that year.

They were great memories.

A time when Jimmy Parrish was still lead singer and Stormtrooper were just beginning to become a global success.

Little did they know what the future held for them.

Back then, they were free spirits, young and ready to conquer the world.

As Ricky soaped himself, he heard his phone ping.

When he stepped out of the shower and wrapped himself in a large, fluffy white dressing gown, he reached for his phone and opened the photo Abi had sent. It brought a wave of longing, reminding him just how much he missed her.

Heading to the room's private bar, he poured himself another Jack Daniel's on the rocks for a final nightcap. To distract himself from thoughts of Abi, he picked up the book he had bought in the hotel shop yesterday – the latest offering from James Patterson. This man had churned out more books than Ricky had written songs.

Ricky found it ironic that these days, after a gig, he was in bed with a book instead of out partying the night away like he used to. Hardly the rock god image, was it?

In recent years, he struggled with crowds and strangers asking for photos or autographs, a challenge that traced back to Ruma. He had developed a small, trusted circle of friends and colleagues and rarely ventured beyond that. In their company, he felt safe.

After half an hour and with his glass empty, he felt his eyelids growing heavy.

He had managed the first chapter.

He put the book and glass on the nightstand, switched off the light and settled down. The bed was as big as a football pitch and felt empty.

He contented himself with the thought that soon Abi would be back to fill it.

As he began to drift off, a knock on the door startled him.

At first, he thought he imagined it.

He lay still as his brain processed the information.

He was sure it was a knock at the door.

Getting out of bed, he padded across the deep pile of the carpet and looked through the spyhole in the door. He could see nothing.

Only management staff or Cecil would come to his room at this time of night and it would have to be an emergency.

For a moment, Ricky thought there might be a fire.

He felt slight panic rise up inside of him.

Gingerly, he slipped the safety chain and opened the door.

He glanced up and down the corridor. It was empty.

Strange.

There were no alarms sounding. In fact, it was totally silent, although he thought he heard a lift ping somewhere.

There was a security desk at the far end of the hall by the elevators set up by the hotel for his safety. Unless you were authorised and wearing a lanyard as part of his team, you had no chance of accessing this floor.

Ricky then looked down and he saw it.

A single red rose and a white card.

He bent down and picked them both up.

He raised the rose to his nostrils. The fragrance was strong and fresh.

He glanced down the corridor once more. It was empty.

Ricky now read the message on the card.

It was neatly printed and said:

For Ricky, from your biggest fan x

***

The redhead regarded her reflection in the full-length mirror in her room. She was looking good. Her make-up was flawless and the red Jasper Conrad dress she wore fitted her perfectly.

She was ready to dance the night away at Zouk nightclub at Resorts World. She loved it there. Holding the title of Sin City's largest and most expensive development in nearly two decades, Zouk offered partygoers an elevated, immersive nightlife experience, complete with one of the best DJ rosters in Vegas.

As she applied lip gloss, she smiled to herself.

The little gift to Ricky had been ideal. A starter, if you like. A token of her love.

After her recent visit to the UK and Ruma Island, she was straight back on a plane to the United States as she couldn't miss out on the opportunity to see Ricky in the flesh, so to speak, at his residency in Las Vegas.

She was fortunate to have booked a room in the Sunset Hotel where he performed nightly.

What a treat. She wouldn't miss a performance.

She wanted Ricky to know she was his biggest fan and she was determined that he would know this. He had to know this before he made a terrible mistake of marrying that whore Abigail Frost.

She had hidden her true love for Ricky for far too long. It was now time to let him know how she felt.

Chapter 3

Ricky was lost in the fog that swirled around him. Tendrils of mist reached out like ghostly fingers trying to envelope him.

Somewhere behind him, he heard footsteps getting closer. Then he heard it – the unmistakable roar of a chainsaw starting up.

The noise chilled him to the bone.

His pursuer was getting closer and ready to extract out some warped revenge.

He had to keep going. He couldn't afford to stop. If he did, he would almost certainly die, just like the others.

He ran on blindly, stumbling on the uneven stony ground of the island.

Somewhere up ahead, he could hear the howls of the island cats.

The fog was now so thick he couldn't see a thing. Yet the footsteps behind him grew closer and the drone of the chainsaw louder.

Ricky was aware of the cliffs and how precarious they were. He hoped that he had not strayed too far from the main track.

Suddenly, Ricky stepped out into emptiness. He clawed desperately, but only felt fresh air.

Somewhere below him, he heard the crashing of waves on rocks.

Dear God, he had stumbled off the edge of the cliff and was plummeting to his death.

As he fell, he saw the faces of his band smiling out at him from the fog.

Rory, Marshall, Erik, Ray. They all reached out, attempting to pull him towards them.

Then, the face of former manager, Bernie Garvey, appeared. He spoke.

"Come with us, Ricky. We all miss you."

But this could not be. They were all dead.

Was this their spirits taking him to the after world?

No. He didn't want to die. He didn't want to go with them.

They suddenly faded away, and through the fog emerged the raging ocean, drawing closer and closer.

As Ricky was bracing himself to hit it, the ocean parted and Jimmy Parish leapt up and opened his arms.

"Come with me, Ricky. Come to a watery grave, just as I did."

"Noooo!" screamed Ricky.

He woke with a start. He was lying on top of his bed bathed in a sheen of sweat, even though the air conditioning was on.

His heart pounded like a triphammer and it took him a few moments to orientate himself.

He then realised where he was and that he had been having a nightmare.

Ricky looked at the luminous dials on his watch.

It was 7.30am.

The room was in complete darkness due to the blackout curtains that kept Las Vegas's desert sun from burning through the windows.

He lay still, regaining his composure.

The nightmare had been so real.

Nearly three years since Ruma Island, the nightmares still haunted him, each one more terrifying than the last.

Ricky sometimes questioned whether he should still be alive or if he should have died on that island with the rest of the band and crew.

He slowly got up and grabbed a remote control, pressed a button and the curtains automatically opened, letting in the light.

He felt better for that.

God, he needed a drink and it had to be something stiffer than water.

Ricky headed for the bar.

A Bloody Mary would do the trick.

That's when his eye caught sight of the rose and card that he had placed there last night.

It still puzzled him how it had come to his door.

He would check with Gabriel later.

There was no way anybody who didn't have clearance could get to this floor as it was all booked out to him and his management team.

Plus, any gifts that fans threw on stage or gave to the team ended up with Janice Strickland, his PA. There was a special room dedicated to them. Nothing personally came to him.

He was unnerved to think a fan could have got so close to him without detection.

There must be a simple explanation for what happened. Well, he hoped there was; otherwise, it was unacceptable.

He tossed ice in a tall glass and then mixed the vodka, tomato juice and a touch of Tabasco sauce in a cocktail shaker. He rigorously shook the contents and then poured them into a long glass.

He knew Abigail would be tutting at him if she saw him drinking this early in the morning as she had helped him cut right back on the alcohol.

Ricky was watching his weight and his health now that he was in his mid-60s.

Nothing was taken for granted these days.

His good friend Lemmy Kilmister of Motörhead had suddenly passed away at 70 in 2015, and then Marvin Lee Aday, known as Meat Loaf, had died in 2022. Both losses had shaken him deeply at the time.

When you were young, you thought you were invincible and nothing could stop you. But the body can only take so much abuse until it begins rebelling.

He saw it happen tragically to his own friend Jimmy Parrish. The once iconic singer had begun to fall apart in front of the band's eyes through a mixture of booze and coke taken to excess.

Although things ended acrimoniously between them, Ricky still missed the Jimmy Parrish he had first met all those years ago, when they both dreamed of creating the best rock band in the world.

For a while, they had been good friends until everything fell apart and Ricky discovered that Jimmy had been living a lie and hiding secrets. This was long before his addictions tore the band apart.

Walking over to the window, Ricky looked out onto Flamingo Road with its busy traffic steadily building. People were heading downtown or further out of the city to work.

He had read in a magazine recently that Las Vegas has been the 7th fastest-growing city in the country for over the past three years. The city offered good jobs, an entertaining lifestyle and a booming housing market, attracting increasing numbers of people and businesses.

The Las Vegas population in 2024 was nearly 3 million. This was a remarkable transformation for a city that started as a small desert town of 110 acres in 1905.

Ricky now switched on the television to watch the weather forecast. The temperature was already in the 20s. This time of year, it could average 38 degrees come afternoon.

Thank the Lord for air con.

Ricky took another mouthful of his drink. It tasted good. Putting the half empty glass on the bar, he decided to hit the shower. His t-shirt was soaked and clinging to him. The water would hopefully also clear his head of the faint traces left of the nightmare.

Dropping his boxers and pulling off his shirt, he entered the cubicle and turned on the massive jets of water. Water shot out like a downpour in the rainforest.

God, that felt good.

The warm water began to soothe away the tension in his body and Ricky found himself singing 'Viva Las Vegas'.

Ten minutes later, dried and refreshed, Ricky walked back into the bedroom.

He regarded his naked body in the full-length mirror.

Although advancing in age, he had still managed to keep in reasonable shape. Most mornings found him swimming or in the gym.

The lifestyle of a rock god was long gone. Well, nearly.

These days, everything was in moderation.

At one time, he could have given Ozzy a run for his money.

He now looked at the bullet wound scar in his left thigh – a gift from Sydney Rose.

Next, he inspected his right ear. The tip was missing, but his hair concealed it. This had been the result of a machete attack by Noah Rose.

In a way, he was fortunate. He had got off lightly compared to his friends.

He walked over to the bar and retrieved his drink.

As he picked it up, he noticed the glass was now empty. He was positive that he didn't finish it, or did he?

Ricky quickly surveyed the room, wondering if a cleaner had let themselves in while he was in the shower and taken liberties with his drink. The room was empty, and everything seemed in order. He approached the door, finding it firmly shut.

He suddenly became very aware that he was naked and felt exposed.

He put the glass down and moved to his wardrobe to get dressed. His body had suddenly become flooded with adrenaline and he felt wired.

Ricky put on a vest top and shorts, then slipped his feet into some sandals.

He felt better for being dressed, but was still spooked.

He decided to head off to the hotel's indoor swimming pool to swim 20 lengths before breakfast.

As he picked up his room card, he glanced around the room once more. He couldn't shake off that feeling that somebody had been in here.

He thought he smelt a very faint hint of perfume hanging in the air that he was familiar with. Was somebody playing a trick on him? One of the crew on a wind-up? Or maybe he was letting his imagination run riot.

Chapter 4

Ricky made his way along the corridor towards the elevator. He glanced at the security desk and noted it was empty. No guard was sat there. Something else to bring up with the management team.

He got into the lift and headed down to the basement where the pool was situated.

He could have knocked up Cecil to come with him, but he thought he would let the big man sleep. He would be fine on his own. He didn't want to be seen to be overreacting.

He had only recently got back into swimming with the help of Abigail.

Since he came across the bodies of Jude Green and Kerry Piper floating dead in the pool at *An Diadan*, the thought of getting into the water sent shivers up his spine.

The two co-record producers had been so young to have their lives savagely torn away from them.

Since that night, Ricky couldn't bear the thought of water, especially alone. However, Abigail, a keen swimmer, had slowly coaxed him back in, month by month. Now, he felt much better about it, but he knew he could never completely erase those haunting images from his mind.

Back in the UK, his 12-bedroom mansion home in Berkshire had its own Olympic-size pool. He hadn't used it up to a week before flying out to America.

He hadn't gone near a hot tub either since Ruma.

He had arranged with the hotel management for him and his team to exclusively have use of the pool from 6.00am to 7.00am.

A few hotel staff manned the entrance to the pool, allowing privacy to swim.

The pool itself was Olympic size and a deep green colour. The sound of the US band Boston's 'More Than a Feeling' was being piped through the sound system.

The place was empty.

Feeling more relaxed, he dropped his towel and vest on one of the poolside loungers and kicked off his sandals. He slipped on his goggles and swimming hat and dived in at the deep end and began front crawl.

In the pool, he felt anonymous. Not a rockstar, just another swimmer. He liked that.

Once Ricky got going, he was pretty relentless at firing out the lengths.

At number 10, he changed to breaststroke and still kept up a decent pace.

Finally, when he hit 20, he stopped and caught his breath, before pulling himself out of the pool.

He smiled as he now heard an old Stormtrooper record playing.

The track was from their fourth album *Riding Shotgun*. The song was their number one single 'Burning Ambition'.

Although Rick had sung it himself dozens upon dozens of times, the song was originally written and sung by Jimmy Parrish in the Mark 1 line-up of the band.

His thoughts went to Jimmy again.

Jimmy had once been the most flamboyant frontman out there, perhaps with the exception of Queen's Freddie

Mercury, but his addictions had ultimately finished him at a young age. Far too young.

Ricky hadn't been able to help Jimmy as it all began to unravel and secrets long buried started to surface. Dark secrets.

It now seemed a lifetime away.

Walking back to his lounger, he picked up his towel and dried himself off.

He then reached for his vest, but it wasn't there.

Ricky looked under the lounger in case it had fallen off, but there was no sign of it.

He surveyed the pool area.

The loungers nearby were devoid of any clothing.

He now looked towards the exit and caught a fleeting glimpse of somebody leaving through the door. A flash of red.

They had their back directly to him and Ricky couldn't see them clearly.

A woman?

He thought about going after whoever it was, but what was he going to say?

Embarrass himself more like by asking, "Have you nicked my vest?"

Oh well, it was nothing special. Why worry?

Probably a fan that got wind he was using the pool at this time.

No matter how tight security was, somebody always slipped through or paid a few dollars to slip through.

Ricky thought back to the rose last night.

Was that how somebody got to his door?

He slipped on a complimentary white dressing gown.

This, in turn, made him think about the mystery of the drink this morning.

Suddenly, Ricky felt a little unnerved again and isolated down here.

Slight panic began to rise inside.

Too many coincidences?

He instantly recalled the breathing exercises he had been taught to calm his anxiety.

Ricky sat down on the lounger, closed his eyes and went through a series of rhythmic breathing.

Soon, he felt better, but wanted to leave the isolated poolside as quickly as possible.

Outside, he asked one of the security guards if anyone had entered the pool while he was using it. The guard replied that he hadn't noticed anyone, though he and his colleague had briefly left their post to handle a potential fire breach, which turned out to be a false alarm caused by someone smoking in the restrooms.

Ricky nodded and made his way back to the elevators.

As he drew closer, he caught a glimpse of someone slipping inside the lift just as the doors closed and it began to rise. He couldn't tell if it was a man or a woman.

He watched it go upwards and then stop at the fourth floor.

By the time it got back down to him again, it was empty.

Stepping inside, he instantly caught the scent of perfume and he now knew it well. It was Dior J'adore.

It was Abigail's favourite.

The same scent he had smelt earlier in his room.

Standing in the empty elevator, he still felt spooked.

Therapists had told him that he would never fully get over the horrors of Ruma Island and certain things would trigger bad memories.

On exiting the elevator, he was happy to see the security desk now manned.

The guard on duty was an old timer named Jack Myers. He shared split shifts with a younger man named Danny Westlake who normally worked nights.

Jack was a good soul, but as he neared retirement age, he could be a bit slow on the job.

"Morning, Ricky," he said.

Ricky returned the greeting and considered asking why the desk hadn't been manned earlier, but he decided to wait and discuss it with Gabriel. After all, that was his job, and Ricky didn't want to come off as a prima donna.

He headed back to his room to dress for breakfast.

On entering, he was glad to see everything looked as it should be.

On the top floor of the hotel was a private restaurant called Benny's, which Ricky and his crew exclusively dined at.

Ricky walked in there at 8.30am to see Joey Bruce sat at the table tucking into ham and eggs. Next to him was Janice Strickland, Ricky's PA, nibbling on a bowl of fruit.

She was a slim brunette in her late 30s. Stunningly beautiful, but also incredibly clever and switched on.

At the buffet table was Cecil, who had acquired a huge amount of food on one plate that would have had kept Ricky eating for a week.

Geoff Tindel and Art Fielding were also there. These two men made sure Ricky's set was ready to roll every night.

Both were in their 50s and had been around music all their lives.

Geoff had a bald pate, but sported a beard that ZZ Top would be envious of.

Art had long grey hair tied back in a ponytail and had a bushy handlebar moustache.

A Crosby, Stills and Nash throwback.

They were both masters of their craft and highly experienced.

As younger men, they had both been part of Stormtrooper's road crew, so Ricky knew them well and trusted them.

Finally, Barry Casper, his fine pianist, was helping himself to pancakes and syrup.

Barry was in his early 50s. A trim well-dressed man with a tidy grey goatee. He was classically trained on the piano, but basically could turn his hand to any music genre. Barry had played with a who's who of stars and, when approached by Joey Bruce about playing for Ricky, the man had jumped at the chance.

This was the small and trusted team that Ricky kept around him for this residency.

"Morning, guys."

Everybody murmured good mornings back and carried on with their food.

Ricky went to the buffet table and helped himself to scrambled eggs and steak. He also poured himself a glass of cranberry juice and joined the others at the table.

He tucked into his food. The swim had him famished.

Sitting near to Joey and Janice, he quietly spoke.

"Did either of you deliver a rose up to my suite last night?"

Both looked puzzled.

"Not me," replied Joey.

Janice looked up from her blueberries.

"You know I think the world of you, Ricky, but I draw the line at sending you roses."

Ricky took a sip of his juice.

"I'm serious. I heard a knock on my door way after midnight and when I opened it, there was a rose and a card on the doorstep."

"What did the card say?" asked Joey.

"For Ricky, from his biggest fan."

"I had the usual flowers and gifts sent to me after your show from fans, but they're stored downstairs. There was nothing that would warrant me coming to your room," said Janice.

"Nor me," added Joey.

"Strange..." mused Ricky, "Maybe Gabriel will know. Has he popped up for breakfast this morning?"

"Haven't seen him. But then again, you know he's not much of a breakfast person. Got to look after that figure of his," said Janice.

"I think he said yesterday that he wouldn't be on duty until lunch time, if I remember rightly," added Joey.

Cecil came over to the table. He had overheard the conversation.

"Are you worried about this incident, boss?"

"Not exactly worried, Cecil, just intrigued. When I went swimming this morning in the downstairs pool, a vest I left on the lounger also went missing. Just two very odd occurrences."

"I can honestly say I haven't seen anybody strange lurking around the hotel, or should I say strange for Vegas," replied the big man, "But I'm on it, boss. Maybe I should come down to the pool with you next time, okay?"

"Yeah. Okay, Cecil. I should have told you I was going there, but you know what I'm like. I hate to be a caged animal."

Joey cut in.

"We know that Ricky, but with your past history, it's better to be safe than sorry. You've done amazingly in the last few years and to be playing Vegas at this stage of your career is a bonus. But you, more than anybody else, will know the music business attracts some weird and wonderful people. Look, I'll mention it to Gabriel when I see him."

Ricky poured himself a cup of coffee.

"Also, when I got up this morning to go to the pool, the security desk wasn't manned."

"I'll will look into that too," promised Joey.

"Thanks, Joey. I really appreciate it."

Chapter 5

A few hours later, Ricky was in the Midnight Auditorium rehearsing some of tonight's set. Barry Casper was on piano, while Joey and Cecil were also present.

After the break-up of Stormtrooper in 2000, Ricky had embarked on a solo career and had released a couple of albums which were well received by fans and critics alike.

His set included tracks from these albums, *Cross your Heart* and *Desert Flowers*.

Both albums produced top ten singles in the form of 'In the Name of Love' and 'Twisted Hearts'. These records were fan favourites, but Ricky hadn't played them much in recent years, so he needed to brush up on the lyrics and vocals.

All the songs had been rearranged from rock 'n' roll to a more mellow bluesy feel. It took some work downsizing a stadium rocker to a slow burn ballad, but they had done so.

Ricky's record company wanted him to go into the studio soon to cut an album of 12 tracks to accompany the residency. It would be the first time Ricky would be back in the studio for a while.

In the aftermath of what happened on Ruma Island, Ricky formed another band called Wilder Things. They released one album *New Dawn*. Again, it was successful, but the scars of what had happened ran deep and after a successful debut tour, Ricky broke the band up as he suffered a minor breakdown.

He went into rehab to fight his demons.

In therapy, he realised he had returned too soon and needed more time to heal. So, he put his music and acting careers on hold. After six months, he re-entered the public eye as a stronger, more grounded individual. However, Ricky knew that if you scratched just beneath the surface, the scars were still there and remained painful.

He was taking one day at a time.

The residency was a godsend, and his relationship with Abi felt like a blessing.

As a big star in her own right and financially secure, she didn't need anything material from Ricky, and he didn't need anything from her. Their relationship was built on trust, companionship, and love.

A successful career in your chosen field can bring monetary rewards, but it can be lonely at the top and very difficult to trust people.

You didn't end up with many true friends. Most people in your life had some sort of angle to make money out of you or exploit you.

Some music stars get taken to the cleaners financially and end up with nothing after years of hard work.

Ricky had been pretty astute when it came to money. He put it down to coming from a working-class family, where money was always tight.

Very early on in his career, he set up Wilder Finance Associates. They took care of his money, and Ricky was well-informed about his income. He had to admit that, over the years, he had built a team of good people to work with him.

Ricky and Abi's relationship was based on mutual understanding. There was no pressure or unrealistic demands on either of them. At their age, emotional games were unnecessary; they were both comfortable in their own skins and simply complemented each other.

Ricky felt safe when he was with her and couldn't wait for her to fly to Vegas to meet up with him. He had a special surprise for her in the shape of a beautiful Anastasia 18 carat white gold diamond engagement ring.

He knew this was the woman he finally wanted to spend the rest of his life with. God, it had taken him long enough.

Well, even Sir Rod took three attempts.

Ricky had gone through more women in his time than guitars. Two marriages, umpteen relationships, affairs and one-night stands. All creeds and colours as he toured the world.

Back home, the Staceys, Traceys, Sharons and Kylies all morphed into one.

In promiscuous times, he had been lucky to keep his health. Many others had failed to do so.

These days, he realised he was a lucky man and chose to embrace each sunrise as possibly his last.

Going back into a recording studio on his own was a frightening prospect, but his management team was the best and he knew they would be there to support him. Maybe he did have one more album in him and could be relevant in the charts once more.

"Let's go through 'Twisted Hearts' again, Barry, and then we'll do 'Riding Shotgun' and finish with 'Stand Up and Be Counted'," said Ricky.

Barry gave him the thumbs up and began the piano intro to the first song.

Joey listened intently. Ricky's vocals were strong, the music was tight and his guitar playing was exceptional. Many people had forgotten that in the Mark 1 lineup of Stormtrooper, Ricky had been the lead guitarist, not the lead singer.

The twist to the well-known songs was something fresh and new.

He was pleased for Ricky. The man had gone through the mill over the last three or four years.

Joey had been surprised when he had received the call about a year ago asking him if he wanted to manage Ricky.

At the time, he had just parted company with an indie band called Strawberry Smile who had accomplished reasonable success.

Of course, he knew who Ricky was. Stormtrooper was a band that was held in the highest esteem, up there with Led Zeppelin or Deep Purple. They had been rock royalty.

Everybody, of course, knew the tragic story of the band unless you had been living on the moon.

To work with rock genius, Ricky Wilder, was an honour and a privilege.

They had hit it off immediately.

Both men had spoken about where Ricky would like to go at this stage of his career and Joey had suggested Las Vegas. He had many connections out there in the music field as he had lived in Vegas for some time in the early 2000s.

Ricky was keen and they then came up with the idea of reworking some of Ricky's and Stormtrooper's famous tracks.

It all came together quickly, and here they were.

Joey had worked with some right fucking knobs and primadonnas over the years. It was refreshing to work with an older and more experienced musician who no longer had an ego the size of a football pitch or who demanded only blue M&Ms in their sweet dish and fresh Siberian goat milk to drink or some other pretentious bullshit.

For Joey, working with Ricky was a matchmade in heaven and the Sunrise Hotel was the best venue for the magic to happen.

The set concluded, and everybody seemed happy.

"Time for a spot of lunch, guys," said Joey.

Nobody argued as they left the auditorium.

When they had gone, a shadowy figure crept onto the stage and went to where Ricky had left his guitar. They ran their hand over it lovingly before picking up the plectrum he had been using only moments ago and slipping it into their pocket before exiting the stage again.

Chapter 6

Back in the restaurant, the group tucked into seafood platters and salad. The food was first class. Everybody except Cecil enjoyed a glass or two of chilled California Chardonnay to accompany it.

As they ate, Gabriel appeared, clad in a canary yellow tracksuit and a pair of brightly coloured Nike Air trainers that probably glowed in the dark.

"Afternoon, darlings. And what a lovely day it is! I've had my beauty sleep, done five miles on the treadmill and now I'm ready to roll."

His eyes suddenly caught sight of the Chardonnay.

"Super. I hope you don't mind if I have a little tipple."

Ricky swallowed a delicious mouthful of smoked salmon.

"Help yourself and have some lunch."

"You're too kind, Ricky, love. Maybe just a few mouthfuls then. Oh, I see you have tiger prawns, I do love them."

Gabriel helped himself to food and wine and joined the assembled group at the table.

"Do anything exciting when we left you last night?" asked Ricky.

"What? Me? Not really. Went to the casino and had a few drinks. That's all. In bed by 2.00am."

"Alone?" asked Joey.

Gabriel smiled.

"Unfortunately, Joey, yes. Alone. But I keep hoping to meet Mr Right."

"I thought you met Mr Right when you were with that Brazilian lad, Adriano, a while back," said Janice.

"Oh, him… Better off without him, love," replied Gabriel.

"I take it he wasn't Mr Right then?" asked Joey.

"Oh, he was, but I didn't realise his first name was "Always'."

Everybody laughed as Gabriel raised his glass in a salute.

* * *

After lunch, Joey cornered Gabriel up by the dessert trolley.

"Gab, can I ask you something?"

"Yes, love, as long as it's not for money."

Joey smiled.

"No, you're safe. It's about Ricky."

Gabriel stopped in the middle of cutting himself a generous piece of cherry pie and looked at Joey.

"He is alright, isn't he?"

"Yeah, he seems fine."

Gabriel relaxed and carried on cutting the pie.

"So, what is it?"

"Last night, somebody knocked on his door and left behind a rose and a card reading, 'I'm your biggest fan'."

"Who was it?"

"That's exactly the point. There was nobody there. Plus, nobody should be able to access the sixth floor without proper clearance," said Joey.

Gabriel reached for a fork.

"Of course. Well, I know nothing about it, but I'll check with security and see if the hotel cameras picked anything up. Also, tell Ricky to bring me the rose and the card, would you? I'd like to see them."

"I'll tell him. Also, he told me there was no security on the desk this morning when he went for a swim."

"If that was before 7.00am, they may have been in the middle of changing shifts, but I'll also ask them," replied Gabriel.

"Right. Thanks, Gab."

"My pleasure, dear."

Gabriel wandered off to the table and tucked into his pie.

Joey went to find Ricky.

***

Joey spotted Ricky in the lounge, enjoying a coffee by a large picture window that framed a lush, exotic garden, complete with its own waterfall.

Las Vegas was a city of contrasts. You were never too far from its in-your-face, over the top opulence, but you could also find some truly relaxing and tranquil places as well. You just had to know where to look.

Joey and Gabriel, having vast experience of the city, knew all there was to know.

Ricky looked up as his manager approached, gestured to the window and said, "See that out there. I could be in the fucking Amazon jungle. Who would know?"

Joey laughed.

"Only in America, my friend. We'll have to take a trip out to the Red Rock Canyon on one of your days off. It's an amazing place and is in stark contrast to the Strip. There's so much natural beauty nearby that nobody ever hears about. Great places for the mind, body and soul."

He took a seat across from Ricky.

"The canyon sounds good. Is it far? I'm crap with geography," said Ricky.

"It's just a few miles west of Vegas and covers almost 200,000 acres in the Mojave Desert. It's really a stunning area of worldwide geologic interest and beauty."

"You've sold it to me, Joey."

"Then we'll do it soon."

Changing the subject, Joey said.

"I just had a word with Gabriel. He's going to check the hotel cameras to see if anything will show up on them. Also, he asked if you could bring him the rose and the card to look at."

Ricky nodded.

"I'll do that as soon as I finish my coffee."

He took another sip and savoured it.

"So, he has no idea who it could have been?"

"Nope. He said security would have known if anybody had tried to get to the sixth floor," replied Joey.

He then looked towards the bar where Cecil sat on a stool sipping a coke.

"Maybe you should get him to sit outside your door tonight."

"Shit, Joey. I can't ask the man to do that. I promised I'll phone him if anything else happens."

"Are you okay, Ricky? If you don't feel safe, we can move to another hotel if you want?"

"No, Joey. I'm fine. I just get a bit jumpy still with strangers who are trying to get too near me and invade my private space. That's all."

"Well, as long as you're sure."

Joey got up.

"I'll leave you to it then. I'm on the end of my phone if you need me."

"Where are you off to? To see that pretty little Asian croupier in the casino, no doubt."

"It's purely business. She's helping me improve my poker game," Joey replied.

"Of course she is, Joey. Well, don't keep her waiting."

Joey began to walk off.

"See you later."

He then stopped and looked back.

"On a serious note, the set sounds awesome."

Ricky raised his coffee cup.

"Thank you, my friend."

After Joey left, Ricky refilled his coffee cup and checked his phone for any messages that needed his attention. Fortunately, there was nothing urgent to deal with at the moment. Sipping his coffee, he sat back in his seat and relaxed.

This was the sort of work he enjoyed. It was a far cry from the crazy tours of the Stormtrooper years. There was a time when he lived out of a suitcase, and every hotel room felt like just another temporary home.

One of his classic quotes during interviews was that he had been to nearly every country in the world but hadn't really seen any of them.

The rockstar life had certainly been glamorous and lucrative, but it had also been damn hard work. He had earned his money and fame.

Some music stars of the day didn't know they were born.

He remembered the early years before Stormtrooper, traveling up and down the motorways in a beat-up transit van with Jimmy and a few other guys who changed often. They packed their gear in the back, heading to another pub or club in yet another dead-end city. Sometimes the crowd loved you, and other times you got bottled off the stage.

He recalled one night playing on despite a head wound from a well-timed bottle of Guinness. He pushed through because he needed the money to pay his rent. Afterwards, he had to go to the local A&E and get five stitches in the wound.

If you didn't complete a gig, you didn't get paid.

On occasions, they played two different venues in one night.

Tough times.

He had spent a large part of his life on the road. In the mid-80s, he recalled the band embarking on a 78-date world tour, covering the States, Canada, Australia and Europe. Two and a half hour shows.

It nearly killed them off. The pressure was immense. At the time, Ricky had been carried along on a tidal wave of euphoria and loved every minute, but he was glad those days were behind him now.

For a moment, he felt a wave of melancholy thinking about the band. They had been like brothers, sharing both the highs and lows of rock 'n' roll life. How he missed them.

He missed their banter, their playful bickering and, most of all, he missed Rory Doyle, the bassist. Rory had been the joker in the pack, one of the first people

Jimmy and he had recruited. A straight-talking Irishman, he had a twinkle in his emerald green eyes that could brighten anyone's day. When times got tough, Rory was always there with a quip or a joke to lift everyone's spirits. He could also play a mean bass.

God bless him. God bless them all.

Ricky became suddenly aware that Cecil had walked over to him.

"What's happening, boss?" asked the big man.

Ricky took the last gulp of his coffee. It had gone cold.

"I have to get something from my room to bring to Gabriel. Wait here for me and then we can go see him together."

Cecil nodded.

"Okay."

* * *

Ricky ran his card over the door sensor and went into his room. Shutting the door, he made his way to the bar where he had left the rose and card.

They were not there.

He looked around the room, which had been cleaned and tidied.

Could the cleaner have thrown them away?

He doubted that theory as they hadn't been discarded in a bin but were left lying on the bar top.

As he scanned the room, wondering if he might have misplaced them, he found nothing.

He was confused.

Leaving his room, Ricky met Cecil back in the lounge and they made their way down to the lobby and to

Gabriel's office, which was situated just left of the reception area. He knocked on the door and Gabriel's voice called out, "Enter!"

Ricky regarded Cecil.

"Wait out here for me, please, Cecil."

The Black man nodded.

"Sure thing, boss."

Ricky went inside and Gabriel looked up from his computer.

"Ricky, darling, come in. Do you want a coffee? Something stronger maybe?"

"No, I'm good, thanks."

"Okay then, take a seat."

He gestured to a garish leopard print sofa.

Ricky sat down and Gabriel got up from behind his desk and joined him.

"Joey filled me in on this rose business. Very strange. Did you bring it?"

Ricky shook his head.

"This is where it gets stranger. It's missing from my room. And the card…"

"Missing?" replied Gabriel., "How?"

"I don't know. I can only think that the room cleaner binned it by mistake."

"How unfortunate. So, you have no proof it was delivered to you?"

Ricky shifted uncomfortably on the sofa.

"What about you? What did security say and how about the CCTV?"

"We lucked out there as well, I'm afraid. Security told me nobody came up to the sixth floor and CCTV confirmed that," replied Gabriel.

"That's impossible. Somebody put it there. It didn't appear by magic," retorted Ricky.

Gabriel reached over and patted Ricky on the knee.

"Maybe it did appear by magic as it seems to have disappeared by magic as well, love."

Ricky stood up, incensed that Gabriel wasn't taking this matter seriously.

"Are you suggesting I've made this up or imagined it?"

"No, of course not, Ricky. I was being stupidly flippant and I apologise."

"Other things have happened as well," said Ricky.

"Such as?"

Gabriel was all ears now. He didn't want to upset Ricky, especially since he could see how agitated he was. Given all the shit Ricky had been through in recent years, Gabriel understood why he was on edge.

Ricky told him about the missing vest at the swimming pool and his Bloody Mary being drunk when he was in the shower.

"Maybe it's one of the crew playing a joke on you?" surmised Gabriel.

"If it is, then it's in poor fucking taste. I've had enough surprises and shocks to last me a lifetime. I don't need any more drama in my life."

Gabriel raised his hands.

"Understood, darling. I promise to keep my eyes and ears open. I don't want you stressed."

Ricky relaxed somewhat.

"Thanks, Gabriel. Sorry for sounding off at you."

"All forgotten, dear."

Ricky nodded.

"Maybe I will have that drink now after all."

Chapter 7

Ricky opened his set with a Stormtrooper favourite, 'Tough Love'. It had always been a crowd pleaser.

Each artist had a song that defined them.

In the rock world, it was classics like Deep Purple's 'Smoke on the Water', Black Sabbath's 'Paranoid', Bon Jovi's 'Living on a Prayer' or Led Zeppelin's 'Whole Lotta Love'

In the mainstream, it was Elton John's 'Your Song' or Robbie Williams' 'Angels'.

Although the artist may have had dozens of other memorable songs, there was always one the crowd needed to hear.

As Ricky sang, the crowd were silent. You could hear a pin drop as he weaved his magic. His vocals were rich and smooth, the guitar and piano a perfect accompaniment.

He knew deep down that he was performing at the top of his game again musically. Out on the stage and entertaining the fans was where he could lose himself and suspend reality for a while.

There was a time in recent years he thought he would never go on stage again, but it is incredible how resilient the human body can be to fight back against illness or trauma, be it mental or physical.

He felt he had made great strides and each performance was getting better.

As he finished the song to resounding applause, the auditorium lights went up, enabling him to see the crowd. This was something he liked to do at his concerts to connect with the fans and not just stare out at shadows.

He glanced out and his eyes were instantly drawn to a stunning redhead seated in one of the middle rows, wearing a striking gold off-the-shoulder dress. She was smiling and clapping, her appearance striking in the shimmering golden gown. For a moment, Ricky found himself completely distracted by her presence.

Her eyes bore into him. In her hand, he noticed she was waving a red rose.

As the lights went down, Ricky thought for a few seconds about the rose delivered to him last night.

From your biggest fan.

What were the chances? There were hundreds of people staying in this hotel and many more attending the show who were not even residents.

There must be dozens upon dozens of fans here in Vegas to see him. How he could single out one woman in the crowd and suddenly believe she had delivered a rose to his very room last night was stupid. An outrageous thought. He had let his imagination get the better of him again.

Still, there was something about her…

Throughout the concert, whenever the lights went up, Ricky's eyes were drawn to her. There was something strangely familiar about her face, but he was sure they had never met.

As the concert drew to a close, Ricky sang the final song of the evening, a cover of the Bon Jovi classic 'Always'.

Ricky was a big fan of the band and had shared a drink with the boys on more than one occasion over the years when their paths crossed.

As the song ended and the lights went up, the crowd rose to their feet in rapturous applause and cheers.

Ricky regarded the redhead and was taken aback when he saw she was holding a large piece of card reading, "I love you, Ricky. I'm your biggest fan."

She then blew him a kiss.

The lights went down again momentarily, and when they went back up to signal the end of the show, Ricky noticed the seat where the red-haired woman had been was now empty.

* * *

Coming off the stage, a crew member handed Ricky a bottle of water and a towel. He took them and made his way to his dressing room. A moment later, there was a knock on the door and Joey Bruce entered.

"Another great performance, Ricky. You knocked it out of the park."

Ricky took a slug of water. His mind was running elsewhere. The red-haired woman had unnerved him somewhat.

"Thanks, Joey."

Joey Bruce sensed the distraction in Ricky's answer.

"Is everything okay?"

Ricky looked at the other man.

"Did you see a red-headed woman in the crowd. Front and centre."

Joey looked puzzled.

"Can't say I did. Why?"

Ricky explained about the missing rose and then seeing the woman waving one at him and the card.

"Probably a coincidence, Rick. Nothing more than that. I shouldn't read too much into it. Just another fan. That's all. And like you said, room service probably binned your rose by mistake."

"Maybe, but it doesn't explain how I got the rose in the first place, does it?"

Joey became slightly agitated.

"Okay. Worst case scenario, a fan slipped through the net, delivered you a rose and went away again. There was no harm done and security will receive a kick up the ass. Plus, Gabriel is aware of it. Come on, Ricky. Chill out, will you? Go to your room, shower and change, and come down for dinner and a few drinks, okay?"

Ricky still couldn't shake off the feeling of unease, but smiled at his manager.

"Yeah. Okay, Joey. Send Cecil in."

Joey walked to the door and then looked back.

"Trust me, Ricky. Everything is cool."

When Joey left, Ricky sat down on a sofa and tried to rationalise the things that had happened in the last few days.

Maybe Joey was right and he was being paranoid, but part of him was still haunted by Ruma Island and he still had a small niggling voice in his head telling him to watch his back.

Another knock at the door disturbed his thoughts.

Ricky got up, went over to the peephole and saw the massive head of Cecil filling the lens.

He opened the door.

"Okay, boss. Got some flowers here from the fans. Is it okay for Janice to bring them in?"

Ricky's heartrate quickened.

Flowers? Roses?

He got a grip on himself.

"Yes, of course. Go ahead."

Janice appeared with three backstage girls and delivered a dozen or more bouquets of colourful flowers to the room.

"These were from your gold member fans in the front row. I promised I would personally deliver them to you. The girls will put them in water for you here in the dressing room. It'll brighten the place up."

Ricky smiled, surveyed the bouquets and breathed a sigh of relief that there wasn't a rose to be seen among them.

He went back to his room and told Cecil he would ring him when he was ready. He showered, changed and made himself a Jack Daniel's on the rocks.

He plonked down onto the sofa and put up his feet. He was still unnerved by the redhead. He couldn't explain why.

Over his career, he had fans say and do many crazy things to get close to him and the band.

In his younger days, he had done many stupid things by letting fans get near him.

The band was used to being chased by hordes of admirers and having to be bundled into cars to escape them.

These days, it was all so different with social media watching and posting your every move.

He wasn't a great fan of social media and it was something he let Janice deal with.

Fans had chased him all his life and a few had even stalked him until the police intervened. You could not determine their motives or mental state.

After everything that had happened on Ruma Island, he felt it was only natural to be concerned that a fan might have not only breached security but also figured out which room he was staying in.

Security were being paid good money and they needed to sharpen up their act.

He reached for his phone and called Cecil.

He needed some company and somebody to take his mind off things.

Chapter 8

The redhead had left the Sunset Hotel shortly after Ricky Wilder's set and took a cab to the Harley Davidson Hotel and Casino a few blocks away.

She was now sat at the bar enjoying a gin and tonic. Guns n' Roses 'Paradise City' pounded out over the sound system. The dance floor was heaving.

She had changed into tight denim jeans, a black t-shirt, short fashionable leather bomber jacket and killer heels. The perfect rock chick.

She now looked around the place. She loved it here.

Adorned on the walls was motorcycle and rock memorabilia.

The woman smiled as she glanced to her left, where a red Gibson Les Paul guitar was displayed in a glass case on the wall. It had belonged to Ricky Wilder and was used on the album *Riding Shotgun*.

It had to be a sign.

Suddenly, she was aware of a person beside her.

She turned and saw a balding middle-aged man leering at her through drunken eyes.

"Hi, honey, can I buy you a drink?"

The redhead held up her glass.

"Already got one, thanks."

The man was undeterred by the subtle brushoff.

"My name is Eddie. I'm here on holiday from Wisconsin. How about you?"

"The name's Angela and I'm a resident of Las Vegas."

The man's eyes widened.

"Wow! Really? What do you do for a living. Sing? Dance?"

He then rolled his eyes suggestively.

"Or something more exotic?"

The woman called Angela eyed the man named Eddie.

He was like a lot of men that frequented the bars here. On a little holiday without the wife and kids and looking for some action. Pathetic losers.

Of course, for the right money, they could find what they wanted, but she was not interested. She was saving herself for her true love, not some fat middle-aged nobody.

"Take your pick, sweetheart. I guess there isn't much action in the good old Badger State, eh?" answered Angela.

Eddie ran his eyes up and down Angela and licked his lips.

"Not as much as here, I suspect. You know Wisconsin then?"

"No, not really, but I watch a lot of quiz shows. I guess the name came up on there."

As Guns n' Roses faded, the sound of Stormtrooper and the title track from their posthumous album *In the Dying Light* came on.

Angela smiled.

"I love this song."

Eddie cocked an ear and listened.

"Stormtrooper fan, eh?"

"Their biggest," replied Angela.

"I saw them once when they toured the US way back when Jimmy Parrish was the lead singer. It was in Minnesota, I think. I was pretty stoned back then."

Eddie had suddenly become more interesting.

"Maybe I will have that drink now, Eddie," said Angela.

"Yeah? Sure thing. What are you drinking?"

"Gin and tonic, please. Pink."

Eddie got the bartender's attention and ordered the gin and tonic and a double Wild Turkey on the rocks for himself.

He clinked his glass against Angela's.

"Cheers, darling."

"What were they like?" asked Angela.

For a second, Eddie seemed to have lost the thread of their conversation.

"What were who like?"

"Stormtrooper."

"Oh yes. They were great, but it all went down the pan when Jimmy Parrish died."

Angela visibly stiffened.

"What do you mean?"

Eddie took a gulp of his bourbon.

"That Wilder guy wasn't a patch on him. Couldn't take to him."

"Why not?"

"Couldn't sing. I thought he was a bit of a dick. He wasn't fit to shine Jimmy's boots."

Angela's mood darkened.

"You don't know what you're talking about. Ricky was the best thing about the band. He proved it. The band were bigger and better when he took the lead."

"In your opinion, darling, but not mine. It was a bit like when Ian Gillan left Deep Purple and David Coverdale took over vocals. Good singer, but Purple were never the same without Gillan as their frontman. Wilder is a decent guitarist, but can't sing for shit."

Eddie drained his glass.

Angela felt her anger rising.

"He's playing down the road at the Sunset. His set is brilliant. You should get a ticket and watch the show."

"I wouldn't walk to the can to see Wilder. Fucking has-been. He should have died with the rest of the band and put us out of our misery."

He gestured to the bartender for another drink.

Angela swallowed her own down.

"Another, darling?" asked Eddie.

"Fuck you and your opinions," replied Angela.

"Hey, missy. There's no need to get like that. If you've got the hots for old Ricky, you better get on with it because I hear he's marrying that posh bitch off the tube, Abigail Frost, very soon."

Angela was now seething.

"That's all talk. There's no proof in the rumour."

"It'll happen, mark my words. Even if you are Wilder's biggest fan, he doesn't give a fuck about you, sweety. What have you got that Miss 'Goody Two Shoes' Abi hasn't got?"

Angela got up from her stool and pushed past Eddie.

"Asshole," she mumbled as she moved out into the crowd.

How dare that bastard rubbish Ricky? What the fuck did he know?

She looked back across the room and saw Eddie stumbling towards the restroom.

Suddenly, something snapped inside her.

Angela felt the change.

A warm glow of rage coursed through her veins

She followed Eddie to the restroom. On the way, she opened her handbag and slipped on a pair of leather gloves, then picked up an empty champagne flute from a nearby table.

* * *

Eddie entered the restroom. It was empty. He staggered to a urinal.

He thought about his conversation with the woman at the bar.

Fucking hell. He was well out of it there. Bit of a mad bitch.

He chuckled to himself as he began to urinate.

Still, she had a nice ass.

* * *

Angela opened the door to the men's room, checked around and then walked straight in.

She scanned the place and saw Eddie alone at the urinal.

There was nobody else around.

What a stroke of luck.

Wasting no time while he was occupied, she moved swiftly towards him, grabbed the back of his neck and slammed his head into the tiled wall.

Twice.

She then grabbed his jacket, spun him around and kneed him in the balls.

Eddie was shellshocked by the ferocity of the attack and already semi-conscious. He was bleeding profusely from his forehead.

He dropped to his knees from the groin shot.

He now looked up through semi-glazed eyes and saw the maniacal features of the woman from the bar.

She snarled through bared teeth.

"How dare you insult Ricky. You know nothing about him. NOTHING. I am his biggest fucking fan. I love him."

With that, she smashed off the end of the champagne flute on the urinal and drove it into the side of Eddie's neck.

Immediately, she stepped away.

Eddie reached for the glass stem and pulled it from his neck. Instantly, blood began to shoot from his severed carotid artery.

He helplessly clutched at his throat and then sank to the floor. He would be dead within minutes.

He watched the women exit the bathroom before he lost consciousness.

Shortly after, he died.

* * *

Ricky sat up in bed with a cup of coffee in one hand and the television remote in the other flicking though the channels.

The sun streamed through the window. It was another scorcher in Las Vegas.

He had slept well, with his nightmares kept well at bay for once.

In the morning light, he viewed the recent strange events with a more rational mind. Maybe he had overreacted to what had happened? Sometimes when things were going well, he had a habit of looking for fault.

He had just spoken to Abigail in London. She was staying at the Ritz Hotel and was relaxing in a luxurious bath before retiring to her bed.

The filming was all going well and on schedule, so she was almost 100% sure she would be in Las Vegas for Friday.

This was music to Ricky's ears. He couldn't wait to pop the question to her.

As he flicked through the channels, suddenly something caught his interest on *Fox5* Vegas News Station.

He saw the exterior of the Harley Davidson Hotel and Casino, where a female news reporter solemnly reported a murder in the hotel restrooms in the early hours of the morning. A 55-year-old man named Edward Bryson from Wisconsin had been found dead on the floor of the men's restroom, having been stabbed in the neck.

It then flashed to an earlier interview with a man named Jose Monaro, a resident in the hotel who came across the body.

Police had no further reports at present.

Ricky flicked to another channel to a rerun of *Frasier*.

Murder in Las Vegas was certainly not uncommon, but seeing this one was just down the road from the Sunset Hotel tended to make it a bit more interesting.

Ricky turned off the television, got out of bed and changed into his swimming gear. He rang Cecil. Within five minutes, the big man was at his door.

"Ready for a few lengths, Cecil?" asked Ricky.

"No way. I don't usually exercise at this unearthly time in the morning. Are you an insomniac or something, boss?"

Ricky smiled.

"Cecil, when you get to my age, you have to embrace every hour of every day as much as you can."

"Yeah. Well, I'll try and remember that," mumbled Cecil.

Ricky shut his door.

They made their way to the elevator and pressed the button for the pool.

He noticed the security desk was manned this morning.

* * *

As the elevator descended, Ricky spoke.

"See on the news about that murder in the Harley in the early hours of this morning?"

Cecil shook his head.

"No. What happened?"

Ricky related what he knew.

"Probably an argument over money, no doubt. After all, we're in Vegas. Or maybe it was about a woman."

"Fancy yourself a bit of a Columbo, do you, Cecil?"

The big man looked puzzled.

"Who?"

Ricky stared at him in amazement.

"Jesus Christ, please don't tell me you don't know who Columbo is?"

Cecil looked embarrassed.

"Yeah. I know. I know. Isn't he that Italian dude who supposedly discovered America?"

The doors to the elevator opened and Ricky walked out, shaking his head in amazement.

Christ, he was getting old.

As Ricky walked to the pool's edge, he was surprised to see Gabriel swimming up and down the length of the bath. He was doing a pretty tidy front crawl.

For a moment, it niggled Ricky that he didn't have the place to himself, but he soon realised that he was being unreasonable.

As Gabriel reached the far end of the bath, he came up for air and spotted Ricky. He waved.

Ricky walked down towards him.

"Bloody hell, Gabriel. You're up early. What's happened? Did you shit the bed or something?"

Gabriel rolled his eyes in disgust.

"How distasteful, Ricky. If you must know, I had a terrible night's sleep tossing and turning. I gave up hope at around 5.00am and decided to come down here when it was open and burn off a bit of excess energy."

"I take it your night off didn't end with a bang then," asked Ricky.

"So crude, darling. I wouldn't tell if it did. Let's say I had a surprise change of plans. Now if you don't mind, I must take a shower."

As Gabriel climbed out of the pool, Ricky noticed that the younger man's body was completely hairless, including his arms and legs, which struck him as odd. Then he remembered that many professional swimmers did this to enhance their speed in the water, a tip he had learned from Abigail.

Ricky also noticed a small tattoo on the inside of the man's left forearm. He recognised it instantly as a heart entwined with a curled snake, the artwork from the front cover of an early Stormtrooper album titled *Love and Hate*.

"I like the tattoo, Gabriel. I didn't realise you were such a Stormtrooper fan."

Gabriel grabbed his towel.

"Wasn't everybody at one time? After all, you were the biggest band in the world for a while."

As Gabriel began to walk off, Ricky spoke.

"Hear about the murder down the road at the Harley?"

Gabriel stopped.

"Yes, I did. Shocking. Just as well you didn't have your residency there, dear heart. Ghastly place full of losers. Don't worry, Ricky. No harm will come to you here. Uncle Gab will look after you."

Ricky laughed.

"I'm sure you will. See you for breakfast?"

Gabriel waved as he walked off.

"Sure thing. Have a good swim."

Chapter 9

Before late afternoon rehearsals, Ricky and Cecil took a drive out along the Strip and down into Fremont Street.

Named in honour of explorer and politician John C. Fremont, Fremont Street was a notable street in downtown Las Vegas. It was the second most famous street in the Las Vegas Valley, after the Las Vegas Strip.

It was just a stone's throw from the first railway line built in Vegas and where the first phone line was introduced. The first casino, the Golden Gate, was also established there in 1905.

Ricky had an old friend who lived near Fremont and Sahara Avenue. He knew him from the early Stormtrooper days. His name was Max Sinclair, a talented musician originally from Glasgow, Scotland.

On live tours, Max sometimes joined the band for his rhythm guitar skills, but he was also accomplished on the piano and saxophone.

Now at 72, the ravages of drink and drugs had taken their toll, yet he remained a capable player. He was playing nightly at a piano bar called Queenie's, earning tips and drinks.

Before flying out to Las Vegas, Ricky had reached out to Max and promised they would meet up during his stay.

Cecil drove in one of the hotel's pool cars. It was a chunky grey Buick Envista.

The big man's head was nearly touching the roof, and he had pushed the seat all the way back to accommodate his long legs. It was just as well there wasn't a passenger behind him; they would have been completely squashed.

Cecil had been with Ricky since he came to Las Vegas about five months ago. They spent most days together and Ricky had grown fond of the big fella.

Cecil was a gentle giant. Although he could deadlift 400 kg and bend six-inch nails for fun, he was a Master of Diplomacy and rarely had to resort to physical force.

In all the time Ricky had known him, he had only seen Cecil get hands-on once. It happened one night after a show when a large Polynesian man covered in tattoos approached, wanting a selfie with Ricky.

There was a line of about 50 people waiting, and Cecil was keeping a close eye on it. The Polynesian man, having had a few drinks, decided to jump the queue.

Cecil calmly intervened, asking him to return to his place in line. The guy confronted Cecil, who repeated his request. When the man stepped forward again, Cecil pushed him back gently. This infuriated the Polynesian, who quickly retaliated with a powerful swing.

Cecil blocked the punch and stepped in, delivering a headbutt that sent the man down like a felled tree. Without hesitation, Cecil bent down and hoisted the 110kg body onto his shoulder, marching him to the foyer and placing him outside on the hotel steps.

Cecil returned to Ricky and the queue of fans and received a rousing round of applause.

Yes, Cecil was a class act.

With the traffic reasonably heavy, it took about 40 minutes to reach downtown Las Vegas.

Downtown Vegas was noticeably different to the strip. Some areas were sorely downtrodden and many homeless wandered the streets. Prostitution was illegal in Vegas and the whole of Clark County, but it was still known to go on in this area.

Main Street and Fremont Street were generally safe, but if you wandered off them, you may encounter some unsavoury characters.

Yes Las Vegas was a city of contrasts.

Ricky and Cecil found Queenie's at the far end of Fremont Street, nestled between a burger bar and a small, old-school casino. The place screamed 1950s, capturing the vintage era of Sin City—the times of Sinatra, Dean Martin, Sammy Davis Jr., showgirls, and the mob.

The club featured a main stage where nightly acts performed, mostly drag shows, which explained the name. There was also a small side stage with a baby grand piano for late-night performances once the cabaret wrapped up.

Night owls could wile away the wee small hours enjoying a drink and the mellow tunes.

As Ricky and Cecil walked inside, they were greeted by a blast of cool air, a welcome relief from the brutal afternoon heat. Outside, the temperature was soaring to nearly 40 degrees Celsius.

The walk from where they parked had been a warm one It took a moment for their eyes to adjust to the low lighting inside.

To their left, a bar stretched out the length of a London bus. It boasted an impressive line-up of optics, bottles and beer taps. At the end of the bar, propped up on a stool, was Max, reading the *Las Vegas Sun* and sipping on a Budweiser.

Max had a deep suntan and a lined face that told the story of a man who had truly seen life. His long grey hair was tied back in a ponytail, and his matching beard was unruly and unkempt. It looked like he hadn't been long out of his bed.

But when those nicotine-stained fingers strummed a guitar or tinkled the ivories, it was pure magic.

Ricky fondly remembered the jam sessions they would have on stage when Max had been part of the band.

Ricky walked up to the bar and a pretty female Latino bartender turned to serve them.

"Yes, gentlemen? What can I get you?"

"Can I get one Bud, please, and one Diet Coke," said Ricky.

"Sure."

"Oh, and another beer for that old asswipe at the end of the bar."

The girl looked a little taken aback and nervously laughed.

"Coming up," she said and busied herself with the drinks.

Max looked up from his newspaper and spoke a strong Scottish accent.

"I heard that Ricky Wilder, you wee English shite. Don't you come into my house and rubbish me. Otherwise, I'll come up to the Sunset and show you how to really play a fucking guitar."

Then, a smile broke on the older man's face.

"Max, you old bastard, how are you?" said Ricky.

Both men embraced.

"Right, that's enough of the soppy shit and less of the old," said Max.

He then eyed the huge frame of Cecil.

"I take it this lad is not a banjo player in your band."

Ricky laughed.

"This is Cecil. He looks after me in case there's any trouble."

Max looked Cecil up and down.

"Well, Ricky, unless King Kong or the fucking Avengers come looking for you, I guess you're safe."

Max extended his hand towards the big man.

"Nice to meet you, Cecil. I'm Max."

"Likewise," said Cecil, taking hold of the older man's hand.

"Now, sit down on a stool, son. You're blocking the damn daylight out."

Their drinks arrived.

Cecil took his Coke and moved over to a row of slot machines by the door.

Ricky sat down next to Max.

"How are you keeping, Max? Are you well?"

Max smiled.

"I can't complain. Not that anybody would listen anyway. I woke up this morning with my boots on, so I guess I am okay."

"How's Marlene?"

Ricky was referring to Max's considerably younger wife, who he had married way back when he had toured with Stormtrooper and decided to make his life in the US.

"She's been gone a year now, Ricky," replied Max.

Ricky was stunned.

"Shit, Max. I'm so sorry. I had no idea. You didn't mention it."

Max saw the shock on Ricky's face and then realised what he'd said.

"Hell, Rick. Not *gone gone*. She ran off with a fucking roadie from Iron Maiden when they toured here last year.'"

"You alright about that, are you?"

"Well, I won't be buying their next fucking album."

Both men laughed and Max continued.

"Truthfully. Fuck yeah. We haven't seen eye to eye for years. Plus, she's 25 years younger than me. What the fuck have I got to offer her these days? While we were married, I shagged everything that had a pulse too. Who am I to judge? No, good luck to her. I think she's living in Manchester now."

He was thoughtful for a second and then added.

"Hear it rains all the time there, so fuck her."

Ricky smiled.

Same old Max.

Max gulped down his beer and set to work on the fresh one.

"Anyways, I read you might be trotting up the altar again soon yourself. Is that true?"

Ricky took a sip of his own beer.

"I haven't asked her yet, but I'm planning to this Friday when she comes over here. She's filming in the UK at present."

"Well, I'm not the best person to give advice on relationships, but I think you've a good one there, son. Beautiful, smart and rich. The perfect combination."

"Hopefully, Max."

The older man regarded Ricky.

"You over all that shit back on that island? Have you put it to bed?"

Ricky was silent for a moment.

"I'm trying hard, Max, but I still have nightmares and still feel paranoid on occasions."

Max stroked his beard.

"It was a hell of a thing to happen. A God damn crying shame. You must miss the boys. I know I do and I hadn't seen them for years."

Ricky nodded.

"It ripped my heart and soul apart. I miss them every day. It was like losing close family. I never mentioned this before, but when we were offered the chance to record a new album on Ruma, I thought of contacting you and bringing you in, but Bernie just wanted the original band, so I never did. Thank God, eh?"

Max nodded.

"There for the grace of God go I."

The two men drank in silence for a moment. Then, Max gestured to the front of the paper he had been reading.

"See there was a murder at the Harley D in the early hours."

Ricky regarded the paper.

"Yeah. I heard it on the TV earlier on."

Max regarded the television behind the bar and saw a news report flash up.

He called to the young girl behind the counter.

"Camila, turn up the TV, will you, darling?"

The girl did as she was asked.

They listened as a big cop with a vivid red scar running down his left check spoke to the press. His name was Detective Ernest Norton.

"We spoke with the bar staff at the Harley Davidson where the incident occurred, and it seems that shortly before Mr Bryson was murdered, he was seen at the bar arguing with a woman. She was a tall redhead in her mid to late 30s, dressed in jeans and a black leather bomber jacket. It may be something or nothing, but we urge that person to come forward to clear their name. If anyone in that bar heard or saw anything related to this incident, please contact us immediately. We are at present checking the bar and casino CCTV to see if there is any sign of this mystery women. Thank you. That is all for now."

Max turned away from the television and regarded Ricky. He had turned a whiter shade of pale as he stared at the screen.

"Hey, Rick, old son. You okay? You look like you just saw a ghost."

Ricky turned slowly towards his old friend and forced a smile to his lips.

"I'm fine, Max. Probably a bit too much sun. You know us Brits aren't used to it."

Max sensed Ricky was lying, but he didn't push it.

Ricky finished his beer.

"Listen, after my show on Friday, I'll come down here to see you play and I'll bring Abi with me. How does that sound?"

Max clapped Ricky on the shoulder.

"Thats fine by me, Rick. I look forward to it."

Ricky got up from his seat and gestured to Cecil.

He turned back to Max.

"Take it easy, my friend, and see you soon."

Max studied Ricky's face. There was a bit more colour back in it.

"You too Ricky. Sure everything is alright?"

Ricky placed down a twenty-dollar bill for the drinks.

"Everything is fine."

Max watched Ricky leave.

He knew he was on his fourth Bud of the day, but his judgement was still sound. Something in that news report had spooked Ricky Wilder.

* * *

On the ride back to the Sunset, Ricky was quiet.

The police had said they wanted to speak to a tall red-headed woman. The woman in the crowd at his show could pretty much fit the bill perfectly.

It couldn't just be a coincidence.

The admirer who sent the rose?

Who was this mystery woman, and did she have anything to do with the murder?

Ricky didn't want to contemplate the fact that there was another killer on the loose and possibly tentatively connected to him.

Sydney Rose had been an evil and deluded bitch that he had been lucky to get away from.

He wasn't sure he was ready for another one.

Ricky reached in his pocket for his medication and dry swallowed a pill.

After a few moments, he began to feel calmer.

Maybe he had got carried away with his thoughts.

The redhead could be totally innocent, but he would keep an eye out and also listen to the news for any updates.

The other burning question was if she was involved, what motivated her to kill this man in the restrooms in such a brutal fashion? What had they argued about that had resulted in his death?

He knew from past experience what the deluded mind of a person was capable of. Christ, he had seen it up close and personal. It shocked him what one human being could do to another.

The unhinged mind unchecked could be extremely dangerous.

As the Sunset Hotel came into sight, he considered speaking with Joey or Gabriel again.

He sensed both men thought he was overreacting to recent events, but this latest piece of news put a different slant on things.

Chapter 10

On returning to the hotel, Ricky spied Gabriel in the reception and approached him.

"Can you spare a moment, Gabriel?"

"For you, Ricky, yes. How can I help?"

"The murder at the Harley. I see on the news the police want to interview a woman seen there at the time. A tall redhead."

Gabriel looked puzzled.

"Okay, Ricky. So, what's your point?"

"I believe she was in my audience last night and I think she's also the woman who delivered me the rose and message. Have you seen her about the hotel?"

"A lot of people come and go here, Ricky. You know as well as I do anybody can pass through the hotel and casino. They don't have to be residents," replied Gabriel.

"I realise that, but this woman is striking, glamourous, six feet tall. She would stand out."

"Ricky, I don't recall such a woman. Mind you, I don't spend much time studying the female form at present. I am in my man phase again. I did see a glamourous redhead walking through the lobby last night, but he also had a beard and a young woman draped to his arm."

Ricky sighed.

"For fuck's sake. Will you take this seriously? If this woman is a resident here, she could be involved in a murder. That means we have a killer in the house and I, for one, am not happy with that, especially if she has designs on me."

Gabriel held up his hands.

"I'm sorry, Ricky. It was insensitive of me, but have you any concrete evidence to back up your suspicions?"

Ricky hesitated.

"Well, not exactly."

"In that case, we don't want to start some sort of unnecessary panic, do we?"

Ricky grew silent.

Gabriel sighed.

"Look, I suggest you ask Faye Conrad on reception. She would probably know the comings and goings of the residents better than anyone. But let's keep things discreet, Ricky."

Ricky nodded.

"Okay. Thanks."

"By the way, the auditorium is all set up for rehearsals when you're ready," added Gabriel.

Ricky looked at his watch. Shit, he was running late.

Joey would be on his case.

The conversation with Faye would have to wait until later.

**

The rehearsals went well, and Ricky worked to keep his focus. Afterwards, he declined a coffee with Joey and headed for reception. He spotted Faye wrapping up a phone call and hurried to the desk.

Faye was a smart and attractive brunette in her mid-40s. Before working at the Sunset, she had done five years at the MGM Grand. She knew her way around a hotel and how to manage frontline service for the residents.

"Hello, Mr Wilder."

"Hello, Faye, and it's Ricky, please."

Faye smiled.

"How can I help, Ricky?"

Ricky asked her about the redhead.

"I don't believe there's a resident of that description as I'm sure I would remember them. But as you know, we have a continual turnover of people through the door every hour. It's hard to keep track of them all."

"I understand," replied Ricky.

Then, Faye stopped talking, thought for a second and then spoke.

"Although, last night around 10.00pm, I stepped out the back of the hotel for a cigarette on my break, and I thought I saw a woman matching that description come out of a side entrance and hop into a cab. I didn't get a great look at her, though. I did think it was unusual as the door she came out of was only for staff."

"Can you remember what she was wearing?"

Faye thought for a moment.

"Jeans and possibly a bomber jacket. Leather maybe."

"Do you know what cab she got into by any chance?" asked Ricky.

"Yes, it is one of our regulars here. Dwight Fielding of Apex Taxis. You know the bright red one," said Faye.

Ricky felt a bubble of excitement in his stomach.

"Do you know if this Dwight is working today?"

"I should think so. He's usually here 6 out of 7 evenings."

"Fantastic. Thank you, Faye. You've been most helpful. How about a couple of tickets to my show?"

Faye smiled.

"That's so kind of you and I'm a big fan, but my 15-year-old daughter would die for tickets to see Adele."

Ricky smiled.

"As gutted as I am to be rejected, I will see what I can do."

Faye leant over the counter and kissed Ricky on the cheek.

"Thank you so much, Mr Wild… I mean, Ricky."

***

Ricky walked out the revolving doors of the hotel into an instant blast of hot desert air.

Slipping on his sunglasses, he did his best to keep in the shade as he walked around to where the taxis waited for their fares. There were a few nudges and whispers as the drivers spotted Ricky walking towards them.

"Hi, guys. I wonder if you can help?"

"Holy shit, it's rock god, Ricky Wilder," said a large, balding man who spoke between mouthfuls of a huge hamburger. "You name it, partner. Do you need a lift? The name's Brad."

Ricky shook his head.

"No thanks, Brad. I'm looking for a Dwight Fielding. Is he about?"

Brad looked at the driver next to him.

"Joe, have you seen Dwight?"

The man named Joe stopped wiping his windshield with a cloth.

"Yeah. He has just taken a fare to the airport. Shouldn't be too long."

"Great. Thank you. I'll hang out here with you boys and wait for him, if you don't mind."

"Hell no, man. We don't mind," replied Brad, "Maybe while you wait, we could all get a selfie. What do you say?"

* * *

Ten minutes later, Dwight Fielding pulled in and stepped out of his car. In his late 20s, he stood six feet tall with a fit, muscular build, accentuated by a tight blue t-shirt that showcased his gym physique.

Ricky approached him.

"Excuse me, are you Dwight Fielding?"

The younger man studied Ricky for a moment, then glanced up at the billboard above the hotel before returning his gaze to Ricky.

His features broke into a grin.

"Shit, you're that dude on the billboard. Right?"

Ricky smiled back.

"Yep, that's me."

Ricky extended his hand.

"Ricky Wilder."

"Never met a full-on rockstar before. I've had a few celebs in my cab over the years, but no rockstars. Do you need a lift?"

"I would like to ask you something, Dwight, if that's okay."

"Fire away, man. What do you need?"

"I believe last night around 10.30ish, you picked up a tall, red-haired woman from here. Am I right?" asked Ricky.

Dwight looked to the sky as if the answer might be floating on a cloud.

"Yeah, I sure did. The lady's name is Angela. A stunner without a doubt."

Ricky felt his pulse race.

"Where did you take her, if I may ask?"

"It was the Harley D."

"You sure?" asked Ricky.

Dwight seemed offended.

"Hell yeah, brother. I'm sure. I do this for a living."

Ricky held up his hands.

"Sorry Dwight. I didn't mean anything by it."

The younger man's tone softened again.

"Alright then. It was definitely the Harley D."

"Have you picked her up before?" asked Ricky.

"Yeah, a few times. Usually, she goes to Resorts World; she mentioned she likes dancing at the Zouk nightclub. Occasionally, she hits up the Harley D, and sometimes the MGM."

Ricky pondered this information and then asked.

"And you always pick her up from here?"

"Yep."

"Have you ever dropped her back here."

"No. I never have."

"How long have you been picking her up."

Dwight thought for a moment.

"On and off six months or so."

"Did she say she worked at the Sunset or if she was a resident?"

"No, man. She never speaks about anything personal. I've tried to strike up conversations, but she doesn't seem too talkative."

Ricky pondered this and then asked.

"How did you get to know her name?"

"It's the name she gives when she books the taxi," replied Dwight.

"Any surname?"

"Not that I know of. I just know her as the redhead called Angela."

"Tell me, Dwight… does she go out on a particular night or is it just random?"

"They appear to be random. Definitely no set pattern."

"Can you recall what she was wearing?" asked Ricky.

"Well, if she's going to Resorts World, it's all glamour and posh frocks. If it's the Harley, then she's all rock chick. Leather and denim."

This matched Faye's description as well as the details the detective had provided on television.

Ricky reached in his pocket and produced a fifty-dollar bill, which he passed to Dwight.

"Thanks, Dwight. You've been most helpful."

The man accepted the bill and put it into his jeans pocket. He fistbumped Ricky.

"If you happen to get another booking from her, could you do me a favour and let reception know? Just have them forward the message to me."

Dwight smiled.

"Have you got the hots for this chick or something?"

Ricky smiled back and thought quickly of a cover story.

"No. I heard she was a good backing singer and I was going to offer her a job."

Dwight chewed this over and then spoke.

"You got a deal."

As Ricky went to walk away, Dwight called out to him.

"Hey, brother. I'm not really into rock music myself. I'm more of an R&B man."

Ricky smiled.

"Don't worry, Dwight, I won't hold that against you."

Dwight looked at him, the joke going over his head.

"Just so I tell my pals when we meet up, are you the guy who sung 'Living on a Prayer'?"

Ricky laughed.

"I wish I had been, but no, that's somebody else. I was in a band called Stormtrooper. Check us out on YouTube.

Dwight waved.

"Will do."

* * *

Ricky stepped back inside to reception, grateful to be back in the cool air. He reflected on the conversation he had just had, considering the implications of what he had learnt.

He was convinced that the woman in the cab was the same one the police wanted to speak to from the Harley.

This woman could still just be an innocent party, but Ricky had a strange feeling about the whole thing.

He knew Gabriel probably thought he was being paranoid and overreacting, but he couldn't shake off the feeling of dread inside.

Dwight mentioned he had been picking up Angela from the hotel for six months, so logically, she couldn't be a resident or just a casual holidaymaker.

Either this person lived in Vegas and liked to frequent the Sunset or they worked here.

The second option didn't ring true with Ricky as surely one of the hotel staff, particularly Faye, would know.

The fact that this woman had been dropped off at the Harley Davidson Hotel and Casino made it highly probable she was the redhead seen talking to the deceased man at the bar.

If this was also the woman from his show who had given him the rose, he might have a serious problem on his hands. The issue was, he had no real evidence to support his suspicions, and given his past history, would anyone even believe him?

Rick began to sense an uncomfortable feeling of panic rising inside him. Surely to God he wasn't going to become entangled in something sinister once again?

The life of a rockstar always appeared an idyllic one. Play your music to adoring fans and earn untold riches. Have as much booze, drugs and sex as you could handle. What's not to like?

The other side of the coin was you were forever living in a fishbowl. You had little or no privacy. Plus, some fans could be obsessive. They would find out every little thing about you and invade your private life as if it was a given because they followed your music.

In the early days of Stormtrooper's fame, mass fan hysteria was the norm, but the band was mostly shielded from this. Later on, when social networks appeared, it was easy for fans to find ways of contacting their idols. Many trolled them relentlessly.

Most were harmless, but there was the odd one who could be dangerous. Look at what happened to John Lennon in December 1980.

A good management team would work around the clock to fend off unwanted attention, but every now and then, somebody would slip through the net.

Did this redhead, who might be connected to the murder at the Harley, also have a connection to him? Somebody again from his past?

The thought filled him with dread.

He spied Cecil walking towards him. Pretty hard not to spot him really.

"What's happening, boss?"

"Nothing much, my friend. Take a few hours off. I'm staying in the hotel. I'll see you before the show."

Just then, a group of women approached Ricky. They were all pretty merry, carrying multi-coloured cocktails in their hands.

A blonde lady called out.

"Ricky, darling, can we get a photo?"

Cecil stepped in front of them.

He knew his boss struggled these days with strangers getting close to him. Since Ruma Island, Ricky had got a little jumpy around fans.

Cecil drew himself to his full height.

"Ladies, Mr Wilder is enjoying some downtime. Please respect that."

The blonde tutted.

"But we're his biggest fans. We're long-term members of the Wilder fan club. We've come all the way from Ohio to see his show."

Cecil went to speak again, but Ricky interrupted.

"It's okay, Cecil. Let them have their photo."

The big man regarded Ricky.

"Are you sure?"

Ricky nodded.

"Yeah, it's okay."

Cecil stepped to one side and the women came forward like a swarm of bees. Ricky drew a deep breath and pushed down his feelings of anxiety.

"Okay, ladies. Be gentle."

Once the photo was taken, the group wanted individual selfies and various bits of memorabilia signed, including an inflatable Flamingo from the hotel of the same name. As weird as that was, it wasn't the strangest thing that Ricky had autographed over the years.

The whole thing now began to get a little overwhelming.

Back in the day, Ricky had posed for thousands of photos with fans and signed just about everything. But now, since the killings, things felt different.

Out of nowhere, Gabriel appeared, like the angel he was named after.

"Right, my lovelies. Time to leave Ricky alone. He has to prepare for his show later and you're holding him up. He's kindly given you enough of his time, so if you follow me, you can all have a free cocktail on the house."

"Thank you," said Ricky.

Gabriel blew him a kiss.

"Any time, Ricky."

He wandered off in the direction of the bar like the pied piper with a dozen women in tow.

Cecil regarded Ricky.

"You sure you'll be okay here on your own?"

Ricky smiled at the big man.

"I'll be fine. Go and have a few hours to yourself."

Cecil grinned.

"Okay, I'm going to hit the gym and lift some iron for a while."

"Yeah, you do that, big fella, I thought you were losing a bit of muscle," replied Ricky.

Cecil frowned and then saw Ricky laughing.

"Very funny, boss. Very funny."

* * *

Ricky took the elevator up to Benny's Restaurant and grabbed himself a roast beef sandwich and a coffee.

The place was empty.

He took a copy of the *Las Vegas Sun* and grabbed a seat.

The front cover had the latest on the murder.

Apparently, the Harley Davidson bar had found CCTV footage of the mystery redhead talking to the deceased Edward Bryson at the bar. However, once they moved away from the cameras, they were no longer picked up.

Nobody fitting the woman's description had come forward.

The police couldn't discount that the redhead may have something to do with the murder, but they had no evidence of any sort. They were still appealing for people to come forward if they saw anything. Up to now, the murder still seemed motiveless.

A background check on Bryson confirmed he was on a week's vacation from Wisconsin. He was a used car salesman. Married with two grown-up children.

His wife told the police that, as far as she knew, Edward had no enemies and was a pretty easy-going man.

If robbery hadn't been the reason for his death, then she couldn't think what was.

At present, detective Ernest Norton, who was in charge of the case, was at a loss to find any leads to the murder.

Murder wasn't common on the Strip; it was more often associated with downtown and beyond.

Norton had worked on some of the worst killings in Las Vegas history, including the mass shooting on 1 October 2017, when 64-year-old Stephen Paddock opened fire on the crowd attending the Route 91 Harvest music festival from his 32nd-floor suite in the Mandalay Bay hotel.

He fired more than 1,000 rounds, killing 60 people and wounding at least 413. The ensuing panic brought the total number of injured to approximately 867.

About an hour later, he was found dead in his room from a self-inflicted gunshot wound. The motive for the shooting was officially undetermined.

The incident was the deadliest mass shooting by a lone gunman in American history.

This present murder was different.

A lot of people came and went from Las Vegas all the time. To find the murderer was like looking for a needle in a haystack.

Ricky finished reading the article and wondered whether he should tell the police what he knew. Then again, it was all circumstantial. He himself had no proof. Plus, did he really want to get embroiled in a murder case and attract police and media attention again? He longed for a quiet life with no drama.

Ricky decided to hold fire on speaking with the police and see what developed over the next few days.

The plans he had in place for when Abi arrived took priority over everything else.

It may have been a tad selfish, but it was the most important thing in the world to him at present.

He finished up his coffee and decided to go up to his room for a while.

Chapter 11

Ricky went up to the sixth floor. As he got out of the elevator, he passed the security desk, where a young guard named Danny was sat monitoring the screens of the whole upper floor.

Ricky called over to him.

"Hey, Danny. No sign of the mystery redhead prowling the corridors, is there?"

Danny looked up at Ricky, appearing puzzled.

"Mystery redhead?"

"You know, Danny. The rose that was delivered to my room the other night and nobody showing up on CCTV."

The young security guard remained confused.

"Sorry, Mr Wilder. You've lost me."

Ricky was now perplexed.

"Gabriel saw you the other day and checked the CCTV footage."

"He never checked anything with me. I know nothing about this."

"That's strange. Gabriel told me specifically he went through CCTV footage with you," replied Ricky.

"As I said, Mr Wilder, I know nothing..."

Suddenly, Danny was interrupted by the appearance of an older security guard Ricky knew as Jack.

"I went through the footage with Gabriel, Mr Wilder. Danny was off shift at the time. It slipped my mind to tell him."

Ricky regarded the other man for a few seconds and then smiled.

"That explains things then. And you found nothing?"

"The only people on the tape were security and authorised staff. We found no evidence of anybody coming to your door, sir."

"Thanks for clearing that up, Jack."

"No problem, Mr Wilder. Have a nice day."

Just then, the elevator doors opened and Cecil walked up. He was in his gym gear and sweating. His pumped muscles glistened.

Danny's eyes grew wide.

"Fucking hell. It's the Incredible Hulk."

The men all laughed.

***

Cecil walked with Ricky to his suite.

"Everything alright now, boss?" he asked.

Ricky nodded.

"I think so, yeah. I'm going to get a few hours' rest before the show."

"Okay," acknowledged Cecil, "I'm on the end of a phone if you need anything."

Ricky clapped the big man on his shoulder, before entering his room, shutting the door and locking it from the inside.

Without a shadow of a doubt, he had heard the knock on the door and had received the rose and card, but nothing showed up on CCTV. How could that be?

Ricky also realised it was now only his word that this all happened.

Would the police believe him anyway if he told them his story? Or would they regard him as a traumatised and damaged rockstar imagining things?

He still felt uneasy.

On the strength of this, he checked all the rooms, but nothing was out of place.

He went to the bar, put some ice in a glass and poured a generous measure of Jack Daniel's.

He then ran water into the marble sunken bath, adding the various bath salts and gels available.

Once the bath was drawn, he shed his clothes and took his drink with him as he stepped in and sunk down into the warm waters. The aroma of lemon and jasmine filled his nostrils.

He lay back and sighed.

The warm waters began to work their magic and so did the JD, both helping to relax him.

He felt the tension in his body easing, and with it, his anxiety began to lift.

He began to rationalise that he had a solid team behind him and they would watch his back.

Things would be fine. Maybe he had just let all his old fears resurface.

After his soak, he lay on his bed, set his phone alarm for 7.00pm and soon found himself drifting into a deep sleep.

* * *

Ricky suddenly awoke. The room was dark from the blackout curtains, and he lay still, giving himself a moment to gather his thoughts.

His alarm hadn't gone off yet. Then, he realised he wasn't alone in bed.

He slowly turned his head to the right and saw a figure under the sheets next to him. He couldn't make out who it was, and more importantly, how the hell they had got there?

Panic surged through his mind. What had he done? Had he been drinking? Taken too much medication? He couldn't remember.

Slowly, he eased back the sheets and got out of his side of the bed. He noticed that he was completely naked.

Quietly as possible, he walked to the coffee table and picked up the remote for the curtains.

He pressed a button and they silently slid open, welcoming in the early evening sunlight.

He turned back toward the bed and was startled to see a red-haired woman sitting up in it.

The woman from the audience.

Angela?

She smiled coyly.

"Well, Ricky. That was everything that Angela dreamt it would be and more. How was it for you?"

Ricky was dumbfounded. Inside his head, he screamed over and over, but then he heard music. It was the intro to Guns N' Roses' 'Sweet Child O' Mine'. What the fuck was going on?

The redhead threw back the sheets and seductively said, "Come back to bed, darling."

Ricky screamed out.

"No!"

* * *

He awoke with a start to the repeated playing of his phone's alarm, which was 'Sweet Child o' Mine'.

Ricky instantly looked to his right and was relieved to find the bed empty.

Jesus Christ, it had been a dream.

He breathed a sigh of relief and threw back the sheets.

Fuck, that had been so real. Too real.

Ricky slowly got up and noticed his body was covered in a sheen of sweat. He headed for the shower, but not before making sure his room door was still firmly locked.

As he checked the door handle, he saw that his hand was shaking.

* * *

When Ricky later took to the stage to rapturous applause, he scanned the audience for the redhead but couldn't see her in any obvious place.

In the front row sat Joey Bruce, Janice Strickland and Gabriel Hart.

When Ricky made eye contact with them, they all gave him the thumbs up.

Also in the front row were record producers from Ground Zero Record Company, eager to cut an album of the show and a DVD.

Whatever was going on in Ricky's head, he had to set it aside and deliver the performance of his life tonight. Could he do it?

Ricky acknowledged his small band, then picked up his guitar and sat on a high-back stool. He took a deep breath and played the familiar opening chords to 'Tough Love', and away he went.

The set went like a dream. He had managed to keep on top of things. His vast experience had taken him through.

Afterwards, he met his team and the record producers in the Chameleon Lounge for a drink and a discussion about the proposed album. A date was set for the recording of the show, and everyone present seemed pleased. A contract was signed, making everything official.

Gabriel organised drinks and then excused himself as he needed to make sure the Midnight Auditorium was cleaned and tidied up before shutting for the night.

Ricky felt more relaxed after the nightmare earlier, and after a few bourbons, he began to unwind. The evening was going well; Ricky Wilder was hot property again, enjoying an Indian summer in the autumn of his career. He truly was a Renaissance man, with more lives than a cat.

***

The redhead sat in a toilet stall of the Hakkasan Nightclub in the MGM Grand.

It was 2.00am.

She had been dancing nonstop for over an hour, drinking champagne and doing a little coke.

Now she needed to pee desperately.

Outside, she heard the main restroom door open and the sounds of drunken female voices that sounded like Brits. Her ears perked up as she caught snippets of their conversation about Ricky Wilder's show, which they had seen earlier.

"Just like a fine wine, that man gets better and better with age," one voice announced.

"That Abigail Frost is one lucky cow. That's all I can say," a different voice added.

"I would love to be in her shoes. Imagine waking up next to Ricky every morning. I'm getting horny just thinking about it," said a third voice.

The first woman spoke again.

"I don't know what he sees in her. I've followed Ricky and the band since I was a kid. I'm a superfan, for Christ's sake. He should be marrying me! No one knows more about Ricky Wilder than I do."

They all laughed.

The redhead called Angela clenched her fists in anger.

How dare they talk about Ricky as if they knew him. Super fan, my ass. I'm his biggest fan. I love the man and I will have him. Those sluts don't stand a fucking chance.

She listened again to the conversation, her anger steadily rising. She knew she had to control her rages, but sometimes they were overbearing and she couldn't stop them.

"If you're a superfan, then answer me this, Maxine. What was the first track written for the *In the Dying Light* album?"

The woman named Maxine laughed.

"That's easy, Sonia. It was 'Lost and Found'."

"Christ, Maxine. You know everything."

"Either you got it or you haven't, Emily."

Angela was now enraged.

The stupid woman called Maxine had got the question wrong. The answer was 'Stand Up and Be Counted'.

Christ, Ricky had mentioned that in his show tonight. Fucking idiots.

Unable to control herself any longer, she unlocked the door and stepped out, surprising the three women.

Angela cast a frosty gaze over them.

They were all in their mid to late 50s, heavily made up and desperately clinging to their fading looks with the help of Botox.

Angela, in her heels, made an imposing figure, standing over six feet tall.

"Call yourself a fan of Ricky Wilder? You haven't a fucking clue."

The woman called Maxine was taken aback by the venom in Angela's voice.

"I beg your pardon," she answered.

"'Lost and Found' was the second track written and it was written by Marshall Meyers, not Ricky. 'Stand Up and Be Counted' was the first song written for the album. You know fuck all," snarled Angela.

"I don't believe that's correct. I think…"

Angela cut Maxine down. Her words were like daggers.

"I don't give a shit what you think. You're wrong. I'm Ricky Wilder's biggest fan and you're just shit on the soles of his shoes."

"Now just a minute. How dare you talk to me like that!"

Maxine stepped forward.

In a blink of an eye, Angela opened her handbag and produced a razor-sharp knife.

"Stay where you are, bitch, or I swear to God, I will cut your lying tongue out."

Maxine froze to the spot.

Her friends grabbed her arm.

"Come on, Maxin. Let's go. We don't want any trouble here. We were just having a bit of banter. That's all."

Angela's gaze burned into Maxine.

"Do what your friends say. It's sensible advice."

There was a brief standoff before Maxine backed away with her friends toward the exit door. She paused for a moment, glancing back at the red-haired woman still brandishing the knife.

"You crazy bitch. If you're Ricky's biggest fan, God help the man."

They opened the door and left the restroom.

Angela returned the knife to her bag. She then went to the mirrors, reapplied her lipstick and fixed her hair. She smiled at her reflection.

Next, Angela hastily found an exit and walked into the night just in case those bitches had informed security.

What did those cows know anyway? When the time was right, she would have her Ricky. Make no mistake about that.

Chapter 12

Next morning at 6.00am found Ricky in the hotel pool working his way up and down. Cecil sat reclined on a lounger sipping a large coffee in a takeaway cup and reading the *Las Vegas Sun*. He had purchased both from the lobby. He had insisted on accompanying Ricky down to the pool.

Ricky finished his 20 lengths, got out the pool and joined Cecil on the adjacent lounger.

"Good workout?" asked Cecil.

Ricky towelled himself dry.

"Yeah. It was just what I needed. That kicked away the cobwebs."

He regarded Cecil eyeing the newspaper.

"Anything of interest?"

The big man turned to page three.

"It says here that the police still have no clues in the murder of that dude in the Harley. The mystery redhead he was seen arguing with hasn't come forward. They think she may have been a tourist who has since left Vegas. Detective Ernest Norton, who's leading the case, is baffled. He's struggling to find a motive for the killing. The victim had his wallet, was still wearing an expensive wristwatch and had his cell phone in his jacket pocket, so robbery has been ruled out. Norton urges anyone with information, no matter how trivial they think it is, to come forward."

Ricky thought about the mystery woman who had been at his show and had taken a taxi to the Harley. He wondered if he should disclose this information to the police.

After everything he had been through in the last few years, getting involved with law enforcement was the last thing he wanted. He knew the media would be all over it, looking to create a new Ricky Wilder story and likely dredge up Ruma Island yet again. He doubted he would ever be free of that chapter in his life.

"Hungry, Cecil?" asked Ricky.

The big Black man grinned and said, "Is the world round?"

Ricky laughed, pushing his dark thoughts to the back of his mind.

"Let's go get some breakfast."

* * *

As both men left the pool, they passed the hotel gym. Glancing through the window, they saw Gabriel. He was working out on the hanging punchbag, executing a series of well-timed punches and kicks.

Ricky had learnt some basic martial arts moves for his television role in *Above the Law*, but he could see that Gabriel was a very skilled exponent.

"Wow!" exclaimed Cecil, "That Gabriel is a dark horse, man."

Ricky nodded.

"You can say that again, big man. With all the crap he told us he's suffered growing up, he probably needed to learn how to look after himself."

Both men watched the focus and intensity on Gabriel's face, a stark contrast to the friendly, smiling, and ever-so-camp persona they were used to.

"Never judge a book by its cover," exclaimed Cecil.

Ricky took one more glance and then headed for the elevators.

"I agree. I mean, who would ever believe you're into listening to Kylie and sipping Prosecco while wearing a pink silk dressing gown and fluffy slippers?"

Cecil's face looked troubled.

"Hey, don't even say that in gest, man. It isn't funny."

Ricky laughed at the big man's discomfort.

As they got into the elevator, Ricky told Cecil to go on to breakfast while he returned to his room to get dressed. Once again, Cecil insisted on going with him, but Ricky didn't want to be herded around like a sheep. He assured him that he would be fine on his own.

* * *

When Ricky exited the elevator on his floor, security guard Danny Westlake asked him over to the desk. He was on his own.

"What can I do for you, Danny?"

Danny looked around him and then spoke quietly.

"I hope you don't mind, but after our conversation yesterday, I took it upon myself to look back over the CCTV you asked about. Between you and me, old Jack is coming up to retirement age and he isn't as on the ball as he used to be and can be forgetful, so I thought I would check that he didn't make a mistake."

Ricky was intrigued.

"So, did you find something?"

"Well, yes and no," answered the younger man.

"What does that mean?" asked Ricky.

"I didn't find anybody on the CCTV tape, but I did check the timestamp and from 1.00am to 1.15am, the fifteen minutes are missing."

"How can that be?"

"It could only be missing, Mr Wilder, if it was erased."

Ricky let this information sink in.

"Could it be erased by accident?"

Danny looked around again and then back to Ricky.

"Theoretically, it's possible, but what are the chances that the exact footage from the time you said the present was delivered would be missing?"

"So, you're saying somebody erased it?"

"I'm only surmising this, Mr Wilder. I have no proof. I don't want to get anybody into trouble here."

Ricky raised an assuring hand.

"Don't worry, Danny. I'll speak with Gabriel and see what he says."

Danny relaxed.

"Thank you, Mr Wilder."

Ricky looked over the desk to the back room.

"Jack not in?"

"He's off for a few days of R&R. I'm covering his shifts. I could do with the extra money. I'm getting married next year."

Ricky nodded absentmindedly.

"Oh, one more thing, Danny. Call me Ricky. Only my bank manager and the tax man call me Mr Wilder."

Danny laughed.

"Okay, Ricky."

He then added.

"My parents are big fans of you and Stormtrooper. They were always playing your records in the home when I was growing up."

"That's nice to hear. Do they live in Las Vegas?" asked Ricky.

"They live in Laughlin. About 96 miles from here."

"Well, if they want to make a little road trip up here, I'll have two tickets to my show waiting for them at the box office."

Danny's face lit up.

"Really? They'll be over the moon. I'll give them a call."

Ricky walked off.

"You do that. Catch you later."

* * *

Back in his room, as he dressed, Ricky pondered the conversation with Danny.

He needed to speak with Gabriel, as Jack Myers had mentioned they went through the footage together.

Something about it just didn't feel right.

* * *

He didn't see Gabriel at breakfast, which wasn't unusual; some mornings he skipped it as part of a strict diet he was following.

As Ricky helped himself to coffee, Joey Bruce approached him.

"Don't forget we have the radio interview downtown with KCEP at 11.00am."

"Sure thing, Joey."

"Janice has all the details and she'll drive you down there. Bring Cecil as well in case any fans are lurking about the studio," continued Joey.

"Will do."

Joey filled his plate with hash browns, eggs and bacon and began to head back to his table.

Ricky called out.

"Gabriel been in for breakfast?"

"Haven't seen him," replied Joey.

Ricky grabbed his coffee and told Cecil he was heading to Gabriel's office, urging him to chill and enjoy his breakfast. After taking the elevator down, he soon found himself at reception, knocking on Gabriel's door.

"Come in!" called Gabriel.

Ricky entered.

Gabriel was sat at his desk, also drinking a coffee. He was wearing a red and white tracksuit.

"Hello, Ricky darling."

"Morning, Gab. Thought you might be at breakfast."

"Not today, love. This is my fast day. Only fluids. Got to look after the figure."

Ricky sat down on a chair opposite Gabriel.

"Saw you earlier on beating the shit out of the bag in the gym. I didn't know you were a martial artist."

Gabriel smiled.

"There's a lot you don't know about me, Ricky. I have unknown depths. But then it's different for me. I'm not a world renowned rockstar, whose professional and private lives have been plundered by the media on hundreds of occasions."

Ricky laughed.

"That's true, I suppose."

Gabriel took a sip of his coffee.

"You ever hear of a man named Ed Parker?"

"Can't say I have," replied Ricky.

"The man is dead now, but he was the founder of American Kenpo Karate. He was the trainer of the stars, including Elvis. He was also good friends with Bruce Lee. He was known as the Godfather of American Karate. Anyway, I was fortunate enough to gain my black belt under him before he passed," said Gabriel.

"Wow, that is impressive," replied Ricky.

"I also hold a purple belt in Brazilian Jujutsu and I train with the 10th Planet Club here in Vegas."

Gabriel was thoughtful for a moment and then continued.

"I love the martial arts. It gives me focus and discipline. Somewhere to vent my aggression."

"Well, that punch bag certainly felt that this morning," commented Ricky.

"Yes. Well, love. I'm a little edgy at the moment. A lot on my mind. Anyway, enough about me. What can I do for you?"

Ricky told Gabriel about the conversation with Danny and the missing footage.

"Shit, I thought I covered my tracks," exclaimed Gabriel.

"What do you mean?" asked Ricky.

"This is between you and me, Ricky. It can't go any further."

Ricky nodded in agreement.

"It's Jack Myers," said Gabriel.

Ricky leant forward in his chair, intrigued to what Gabriel was going to disclose.

"What about Jack Myers?"

Gabriel took another sip of his coffee.

"He's nearly at retirement age and he's been in hotel security here in Vegas a long time. He stands to get a decent pension and he has plans to buy himself a little boat and move away to Martha's Vineyard, Massachusetts to live."

"And?" replied Ricky.

"He's shown signs of possibly having early onset Alzheimer's. He's getting forgetful. I'm the only one who he told and I look out for him. He has four months to go in the job. What I'm getting around to was he accidently wiped that section of the tape. He was trying to home in on the corridor because he thought he saw something and pressed the wrong button. When he realised 15 minutes were gone, he confessed the mistake to me. He was most upset, so I told him I would cover for him and say there was nothing on the CCTV that night you asked. I didn't expect Danny to go poking around."

Ricky sat back in his chair.

"So, we're no nearer to knowing who delivered the gift."

"Afraid not, Ricky. I'm sorry for the cock-up. I saw nothing myself."

Ricky sighed.

"Thanks for clearing that up anyway, Gabriel."

"I know it's not strictly above board, but if the hotel manager gets a sniff that Jack isn't capable of doing his job, he will have him out of here. I can't see that happen to the old boy."

"No, you did right, Gab. Okay. Mystery solved. Thanks for your time."

Gabriel smiled.

"For you, Ricky, I have all the time in the world."

Ricky got up from his chair.

"I'll leave you to it. See you later at the show."

Gabriel leaned back in his chair.

"You can count on that, Ricky. I'll be there."

Ricky suddenly stopped at the door.

"I don't suppose there's a slight chance that Jack did see something on the tape before it was wiped?"

Gabriel put down his coffee cup.

"He didn't mention anything to me, Ricky. Besides, the way things are going with him, could we trust his judgement anyway?"

"Still, maybe I'll have a word with him when he comes back from his vacation. It's got to be worth a shot."

"I really think you would be wasting your time," replied Gabriel.

"I appreciate what you're saying, but it'll just put my mind at rest," said Ricky.

"As you wish. But it's getting to the point where old Jack has a job to remember what day it is sometimes."

Gabriel headed back to his desk.

Ricky nodded and opened the door.

"No more strange incidents, I take it?" called Gabriel.

Ricky looked back.

"No, not really."

Ricky left the office, deciding to keep his thoughts to himself for now. He couldn't shake the feeling that his management staff and Gabriel had held a meeting about him – perhaps expressing concerns that stress was causing him flashbacks or making his mind play tricks.

Yes, there had been a time where that had been the case and Ricky had been prescribed 20mg of Prozac on a daily basis to help with his anxiety. But he had cut the medication right back and was doing okay.

Some days, while he was on it, he felt like a zombie. Meeting Abi and landing this gig had really helped; he felt much more like his old self. However, he knew that people close to him would still be monitoring his every move.

After all, everybody stood to make a lot of money, not only from the residency but also the subsequent recordings. He was the cash cow. Nobody wanted him to fall ill again as there was too much riding on him at present.

Ricky was too long in the tooth not to realise this.

That was the music business for you.

Dog eat dog.

Everybody ultimately was looking out for their own interests.

There was an old saying that Ricky recalled.

You are only useful as a person to somebody else as long as you have something to offer.

It was hard to find a true friend that would be there for you in good and bad times, that gave their love and support unconditionally.

The lads in Stormtrooper had been good friends.

No matter where in the world they had been, they would always be there for each other if needed.

Ricky missed their company badly.

But the show must go on.

He made his way through the reception to the foyer to find Janice and Cecil waiting for him.

Chapter 13

The radio interview went well. The woman interviewing him was Kelly Perry. Ironically, Ricky had been interviewed by her mother back in the 90s when they were on a tour of the States.

Glenda Perry had been a well-respected radio presenter with an encyclopaedic knowledge of music. She had interviewed all the greats from Bowie and Dylan to Jagger and Springsteen.

Tragically, she had died in her late 40s in a light aircraft crash on her way from Vegas to Reno. Three others died with her.

She had been on her way to see her favourite artist, Tom Petty, at a gig he was playing there at the Lawlor Event Centre on 12 June 1995.

Kelly, her daughter, took over the legacy her mother had left behind and became a seasoned presenter in her own right. Her specialty areas were rock and country music.

She had prepared well for her interview with Ricky and knew all about him.

Kelly had given Ricky's residency at the Sunset a significant plug, and he was grateful for that.

Naturally, the interview wouldn't be complete without a mention of Ruma Island. Ricky was surprised to learn that Kelly and her boyfriend had recently travelled to the UK and done the whole Ruma massacre tour.

After the show, over coffee, Ricky was intrigued to learn more about the island tour and what it entailed. He shook his head in amazement as Kelly shared the details, her enthusiasm palpable.

"Christ, it never amazes me how some people have no scruples about making money out of other's tragedies and misfortunes."

Kelly gently touched his arm.

"Sorry if I was being insensitive. It must still be a pretty raw subject, even after all this time."

Ricky smiled.

"It's fine, Kelly. No harm done. Hell, I've made millions out of the incident myself. Who am I to judge?"

He took a sip of his coffee.

"Anyway, these trips are sellouts, are they?"

"According to the guides, yes. Fans come from all over the world and they'll do anything to get inside the house. They practically have to nail everything down to discourage souvenir hunters making off with something. The tickets are like gold dust and there's a long waiting list. We applied a year or more ahead of time.

While we were on the tour, a woman decided to stray from the group, which isn't allowed. Apparently, she spent a considerable amount of time in your room. She had no idea there were hidden cameras installed all over the house. She didn't do any harm, but the policy is clear: stick with the group and don't wander off on your own. The staff called her out on it."

Ricky laughed, but he suddenly felt a chilled prickle go across his skin.

"I suppose you didn't find out who she was?"

It was Kelly's turn to laugh.

"No, we didn't, but my money would have been on a rather glamourous American redhead. She was constantly interrupting the guide and asking endless questions about you."

Ricky's mind was working overtime and Kelly's voice was fading out of his consciousness.

A red-haired woman again.

It couldn't just be coincidence.

This woman had to be stalking him.

If it was the same woman who had been seen in the Harley, could she be capable of murder? If so, this person was dangerous.

* * *

On the drive back to the hotel, Ricky decided that he would speak with Joey and try to convince him to see that there could be a connection to the murder and the strange things that had been happening.

Janice Strickland looked over from her driver's side seat of the Chevrolet Camero they were in.

"You alright, Ricky? You've been quiet since you got back in the car. The interview went really well in my eyes. Are you worried about it?"

Ricky pulled his thoughts back to the present.

"Sorry, Janice. I was miles away. No, I'm happy how the whole thing went."

"Were you okay with the Ruma Island stuff? Was it too much?"

"No, it was fine, Janice. Honestly."

Janice nodded.

"You know you can speak to me if you want to, don't you?"

Ricky looked at the younger woman. Janice had been a star since she joined his team. Although she hadn't worked in the music industry before, she took to it like a duck to water.

Before being employed by Ricky, she had worked for a very high-powered business consultant in New York. She was punctual, proficient and a great organiser.

Although they didn't socialise a lot together, Janice was a perceptive individual and knew Ricky inside out. He loved having her as part of the team. She was young and had her finger on the pulse of what was happening in the moment.

"I know I can confide in you, Janice. I really appreciate that."

Ricky then changed the subject.

"Anyway, how's that girlfriend of yours, Carly, doing? When is she going to come down to the show."

Janice smiled.

"I've been asking her for the last few weeks, but she's been busy at the hospital. She's trying to get time off this weekend."

Janice's long-term partner, Carly Dobbs, worked as a nurse at Las Vegas's largest acute care facility on Maryland Parkway named the Sunrise Hospital and Medical Centre. She was a martyr to the job.

"See that she does, Janice. Abi is flying in tomorrow night and we can all go out for a late dinner after my show."

"That would be nice, Ricky. I'll keep badgering her."

"You know what the problem is. She works at Sunrise and I work at Sunset," said Ricky.

"Very good, Ricky," laughed Janice.

Soon, the Sunset Hotel came into view and they pulled into the underground parking lot.

"Thanks for this morning, Janice," said Ricky.

"No problem. Are you okay to go into the hotel yourself? I have some calls to make," she replied.

Ricky nodded and got out of the car. Cecil exited the backseat and joined him as they headed for the elevator. Ricky told Cecil he was off to find Joey and would call him if he was needed again.

***

Ricky found Joey sunbathing on the roof terrace by the pool.

Joey Bruce was a sun worshipper, rarely seen without a permanent tan. He owned a villa in the Florida Keys and took every opportunity to fly out there for a much-needed boost of vitamin D and a break from the madness of Vegas. He firmly believed that sunshine made you feel better and healthier.

Gabriel, on the other hand, had told him more than once that he was a prime candidate for skin cancer.

Even Joey knew his limits, however.

It was 3.00pm and the sun was at it hottest, nearing 40 degrees.

Joey sat under the shade of a large umbrella sipping a cocktail.

He saw Ricky approaching and waved.

Ricky sat on a lounger next to him, also under an umbrella, glad to get out of this sweltering heat.

"Heard the radio show, my friend. First class," said Joey.

"Thanks."

Joey slid his sunglasses up onto his forehead.

"Are you all right, old son? You look a bit down in the mouth."

"It's this business with this damn red-headed woman who magically keeps appearing and disappearing."

Joey sat forward on the lounger.

"What's happened?"

Ricky went on to explain what Kelly Perry had told him. When he had finished, Joey spoke.

"So, you're telling me you think the woman on Ruma Island is the same one you've seen in the crowd here and the one you believe left you the gift outside your door?"

Ricky nodded.

"That's about the length and breadth of it. Also, I think she was involved in the murder at the Harley Davidson."

Joey put up a hand to interrupt him.

"Hey, Ricky. With all due respect, that's a big leap from a possible obsessive fan to a killer."

"Dwight Fielding, a taxi driver from this hotel, told me on the night of the murder he picked up a red-haired woman from here and dropped her off at the Harley. He also told me he had picked her up from the Sunset on numerous occasions. Tell me, Joey, that's not a coincidence?"

Joey leant over to the drinks table and refilled his glass with another margarita.

"Drink?" he asked.

Ricky shook his head.

"Do you think this woman is a resident in this hotel and is stalking you, Ricky?"

"There's a strong possibility, yes."

Joey blew out his cheeks.

"Wow."

He took a gulp of his drink.

"Can you think who it may be? Do you know any red-headed woman? Is it someone from your past maybe?"

"Fucked if I know, Joey. I've met and been with a lot of women over the years. There are also parts of my career that are a blur and other parts lost for good. Shit, it could be anybody."

Joey looked at Ricky. The man looked troubled.

"Do you believe the woman is a danger to you?"

"I honestly don't know, Joey, but I do know she is still out there and I don't know what her motives are."

Joey reached over and patted Ricky's arm.

"Okay. Look, I will step up security and make sure we have extra people close to the stage and in the audience when you perform. Outside that, Cecil is more than a deterrent for anybody. I will make the arrangements now."

Ricky smiled.

"Thanks, Joey."

"No problem. I'm here to help. Now, do you also want the police contacted?"

Ricky shook his head.

"Let's hold fire for now. I really don't want to get them involved and waste their time. Plus, I don't want the publicity."

"Okay. For now, we sit on it, but keep our eyes and ears peeled."

Ricky got to his feet.

"Shit, Joey. I don't know how you can stand this heat."

Joey laughed.

"It must be in the genes. My grandfather was in the Foreign Legion."

Ricky shook his head.

"You're crazy. Anyway, I'm off to my room for a nap and a long bath before the show."

"Okay. Take it steady. And don't worry. I'll sort out security. I promise it'll be tighter than a duck's ass and that is watertight."

* * *

As soon as Ricky had disappeared inside, Joey picked up his mobile phone and pressed a button. Immediately, it was answered.

Joey spoke quickly.

"I need to see you in private. We may have a problem with Ricky. He's raving on again about this fucking redhead."

Chapter 14

Ricky exited the elevator and acknowledged Danny on the security desk.

"Everything ok, Dan?"

The young man smiled.

"Yes, all good. It's been quiet up here. Your room cleaner, Rosa Del Rey, checked in and out with me as per instructions. Gabriel has come up a few times to check all is in order."

"Okay. Great," replied Ricky.

He walked down the corridor towards his room and there he spotted something on the floor outside the door.

His heart momentarily skipped a beat until, as he drew closer, he saw it was the hotel's complimentary copy of the newspaper, *USA Today*.

He bent down, picked it up and then let himself into his room.

It smelt fresh and aired.

The bed linen was clean. The bar was topped up and the bathroom was full of luxury soaps and lotions again. Crisp white towels were stacked neatly.

Everything seemed in order.

Ricky used the toilet and then made himself a JD on the rocks as he casually picked up the newspaper and glanced at the front page.

Its headlines were all about the attempted assassination of Donald Trump.

That said, it was shocking that even in this day and age, assassination attempts were still occurring. Had we learnt nothing from our history?

Over the years, Ricky had played to some massive crowds and had wondered more than once whether there was some lunatic out there with a gun targeting him.

You could never take anything for granted.

As Ricky opened the newspaper, something dropped out and onto the carpet.

He reached down and picked it up. It was a white card. There was a message on it.

His eyes scanned it.

I will be at the show again tonight. Wouldn't miss it for the world. Would love if you would dedicate your song 'Lovin' You Always' to me. Your biggest fan, Angela.

Love and Kisses xxxxxx

Ricky stared at the card in horror.

How the hell had it got into the newspaper?

He dropped the card onto the bar, left his room and headed back down the corridor to the security desk.

Danny was talking to Gabriel and Joey.

They all saw Ricky heading their way.

Joey called out.

"Ah, just the man we wanted to see. We're upgrading security as we speak and we're going to have another person on the desk here with Danny and Jack…"

Ricky cut them off.

"Who delivered the newspaper outside my door today?"

Everybody momentarily looked confused.

"Paper? What paper?" asked Gabriel.

"The fucking *USA Today* newspaper. Who left it there?" shouted Ricky.

Danny spoke.

"The room service person would have brought it up."

Ricky looked from Joey to Gabriel.

"Come with me."

With that, he strode off down the corridor.

Both men exchanged worried looks and followed.

Inside his room, Ricky picked up the card and showed it to both men.

"This was inside the newspaper."

Joey and Gabriel read the message.

"Jesus, I don't understand how it could have got into the paper," said Joey.

He looked at Gabriel.

The other man shook his head.

"I've been up here a few times today. Nobody bar the cleaner was here. She's worked for the hotel since it opened. She's married with three children and is also a grandmother. She isn't your mystery redhead, Ricky."

"Somebody is fucking with me. They know my past and they're playing on it."

"Now take it easy, Ricky. Let's look at this rationally."

Gabriel headed to the bar.

"Let me get us a drink."

Joey got Ricky to sit down on the sofa where he joined him.

"Let's look at what we have got here. We have an obsessive fan. It can't be your first, Ricky. They have somehow cleverly managed to breach security. Maybe they've bribed someone at the hotel to get these messages to you. I don't know. But they haven't threatened you in any way. Nothing for you to worry unduly about."

Ricky accepted the bourbon Gabriel handed him as he joined them.

He downed it in one gulp.

"Joey, you may be right, but with the shit I went through on Ruma Island, you know how paranoid I am about security and strangers getting access to my private life. Part of the deal here was my security."

Joey nodded.

"I agree, and after our earlier conversation, I've spoken with Gab and we are upping it. This incident unfortunately happened today before you spoke with me. I promise it won't happen again. I'll put Cecil in the picture. He'll be ready to do whatever is needed, even sleeping on the couch in here if you want."

Ricky rubbed his hands over his face. He suddenly felt weary.

"Fuck no. I don't want that."

Gabriel put his hand on Ricky's shoulder.

"Ricky, your shows are going like a dream. Sellouts every night. Don't let these incidents ruin it for you."

Ricky looked at both men.

"What if this woman is the same one who murdered that dude in the Harley? What if she's coming for me?"

"Why would she want to hurt you? Her messages clearly stated she's your biggest fan," replied Gabriel.

Ricky chewed that thought over for a moment.

Joey then spoke.

"I will give the card to Danny and ask him to privately run it for fingerprints just in case. Also, if we see this woman in the audience tonight, we will get security to discreetly lift her for questioning."

Ricky nodded.

"Look, guys. I've been keeping this a secret, but it's important you know now more than ever. Abi is flying in tomorrow, and after my gig, I want us all to go out for dinner and then hit a little club I know downtown. I'm going to propose to her. I have a ring and everything. If she accepts, my plan is for us to marry as soon as possible. That's why I don't want any shit going down. This has got to be perfect. Our busy schedules have made it near on impossible to spend quality time together and for me to pop the question. Tomorrow is that moment and it must be just right."

Joey raised his glass.

"Well, nice one, partner. I wish you all the luck in the world. You are made for each other. What do you say, Gab?"

Gabriel was quiet for a moment and then smiled.

"Wonderful news, Ricky darling. I just knew you were up to something."

***

Later that night, just before going on stage, Ricky scanned the crowd from behind the curtain. There was no sign of the redhead.

Backstage cameras in the auditorium sent images to computer screens, allowing technicians to zoom in and out and check the crowd covertly.

By the time the show was set to start, the auditorium was full, but the elusive redhead was still nowhere to be seen.

Ricky breathed a sigh of relief.

Joey patted him on the back.

"Go get 'em, champ."

Ricky nodded and walked out onto the stage.

Barry Casper at the piano opened up with a few bars as Ricky Wilder picked up his guitar and said, "Good evening, everybody!"

* * *

Backstage, Gabriel looked at Joey.

"Is he going to be okay? He got quite emotional earlier on."

"He'll be fine."

"I hope so, Joey. There's a hell of a lot riding on this. There's a lot of money to be made. Not just the shows but the recordings."

Joey turned to Gabriel.

"You don't have to remind me, Gab. I know. I want him in tiptop shape myself. If only we could find this damn woman, Angela, and get her out of Ricky's life."

"Well, darling, that is like looking for a needle in a haystack here in Vegas," replied Gabriel.

"Just keep security on it, Gab. We might just get lucky."

"Will do."

They turned back to the stage just as Ricky finished his opening song to loud applause.

* * *

Later that night back in his room, Ricky phoned Abi and she confirmed that she would be landing tomorrow at Harry Reid Airport at 1.30pm.

Ricky told her that Cecil would meet her at the arrivals gate and he would be waiting in the car. He didn't want to draw any media or fan attention by being seen at the airport.

Abi told him her filming had gone well and she was now looking forward to some well-earnt rest. Ricky said he couldn't wait to see her. It had been over a month since they had been together.

When he hung up the call, he lay on the bed but couldn't sleep.

This was not unusual.

Back in the day, he would be popping some 'downers' – a slang term for a depressive drug that slows down your brain's activity and induces feelings of relaxation and tiredness.

Not these days though.

He glanced at his watch. It was 2.00am.

He knew sleep wasn't going to come.

Ricky dressed.

He decided he would go down to the casino, play on the slots and get a drink. It might help him chill.

With extra security 24/7 now being provided, he wasn't going to wake Cecil.

As he left his room and walked to the security desk, a smartly dressed grey haired man got up from his seat next to Danny Westlake.

"Morning, Mr Wilder. My name is Cody Wilson, part of your security team just drafted in. Can I help?"

Ricky shook the man's hand.

"Hello, Cody. I'm just on my way to the casino. Can't sleep."

"Okay, Mr Wilder. Let me accompany you and I will keep an eye on you downstairs from a discreet distance," replied Cody.

Both men entered the elevator and it made its way to the casino floor.

"Have you been in the security business long?" asked Ricky.

"Five years to date. Before that, I was a Navy Seal. Seen action in Afghanistan."

"I'm impressed."

"You're impressed," replied Cody, "And here I am sharing an elevator with rock legend Ricky Wilder."

Both men laughed.

The doors opened to the clinking and tinging of a thousand blinking machines.

Even at 2.00am, it was still relatively busy.

Las Vegas truly was the 24-hour nonstop party capital.

80,389 square ft of gaming space spread out in front of them.

It was mesmerising.

This area was large, but places like Caesars Palace were even bigger. You needed a map to navigate your way around.

All the casinos were devoid of clocks, so you never knew what time it was – just a ploy to keep you gambling.

Ricky walked around the floor with Cody Wilson shadowing him until he settled on a machine and sat on a stool in front of it.

"I'll play here for now, Cody."

"Fine, Mr Wilder. I'll be close by if you need me."

Ricky hated having close security, but in light of recent events, he felt safer with it.

He ordered a drink from the cocktail waitress who passed by, then slotted his credit card into the machine to play.

Ricky wasn't much of a gambler, which, in some ways, was a blessing. He remembered back in the day when Stormtrooper was on the road; the band often played poker.

Jimmy Parrish was the Maestro when it came to five-card stud.

Ricky was rubbish and lost a lot of money.

The band always took the piss out of him, but he never improved. In the end, he let them get on with it.

Jimmy had even written a song on their second album called 'Five-Card Stud' that had the same vibe as the Motorhead classic 'Ace of Spades'. Ricky never played it live after taking over from Jimmy as the lead singer.

* * *

After playing for ten minutes, Ricky had spent $100 and won back $40. He decided to take a break and sipped his drink.

Ricky became aware that Cody Wilson was by his side.

"Mr Wilder, I have to quickly use the restroom. Will you remain on this machine until I return?"

"Sure. I'll be here."

Cody excused himself.

Ricky sat and surveyed his surroundings, and then he saw her. She was at a corner machine, playing with her back to him. But he was sure it was her – it was the redhead.

Ricky glanced toward the restroom, contemplating whether he should wait for Cody.

But what if this woman just got up and walked? He may lose her again.

He needed to talk, just for his own sanity.

Ricky took a deep breath and got up from his seat. He made the decision to approach her. Maybe he might find out that it was all a big misunderstanding.

Ricky truly wanted to believe in that.

He approached the woman and spoke.

"Angela, is that you?"

Startled, the woman turned around and looked at him.

"No, sorry. My name is Sandra. Sandra Cox. And you are, if I'm not mistaken, THE Ricky Wilder. My husband and I watched your show tonight, and it was excellent."

Suddenly, a middle-aged man appeared carrying two beers.

Sandra spoke excitedly.

"Honey, look! It's Ricky Wilder."

The man regarded Ricky, then his face split into a grin.

"Well, I'll be damned. Have I died and gone to heaven? Shit, I've followed you for years. Stormtrooper are my most favourite band ever."

Ricky was embarrassed, realising he had made a mistake.

He could see now that it was plainly not the mystery woman.

"I'm sorry I disturbed your wife. I thought she was somebody else. Forgive me."

"Nothing to forgive, my man. My name is Harvey and this is Sandra. May we pinch a selfie with you?"

From the corner of his eye, he saw Cody approaching, looking a little flustered.

He turned back to the couple.

"Sure, let's do it."

Ricky got between Sandra and Harvey and the photo was taken.

"Thank you so much. It was lovely to meet you," said Sandra.

Harvey shook Ricky's hand enthusiastically.

"Great to have met you. Wait until I tell my work buddies back in Boston."

The man then leant in close and said, "We're in room 232. We have an open marriage and an understanding, if you get my drift. Sandra would be up for a little fun."

Cody intervened in the conversation, trying to be as tactful as possible.

"Ah, there you are, Mr Wilder. I've been looking for you."

The couple turned back to the machine they were on and Cody led Ricky away.

"I'm sorry, Ricky, but I must insist. You need to stay near me."

Ricky held up his hands.

"I apologise. I saw the red-headed woman and thought it might be this stalker, Angela."

"With respect, that may be so, but I'm the person trained and paid to deal with these problems, not you."

"Alright, Cody. I get the message. Anyway, I'm heading back up to my room."

Cody nodded.

"As you wish. Let's go."

If Ricky had been looking to the right of the casino as he walked to the elevators, he would have seen Angela leaving by a side entrance and out into a waiting taxicab.

She was pissed off that she hadn't been able to attend the show this evening, but she had been grateful of the tipoff. From now on, she was going to have to be more careful.

There would be no visits to the Harley Davidson bar, that was for sure, and the MGM was best to avoid too.

To get her entertainment, she decided to head up to the other end of the Strip and go to the Bellagio or the Venetian. She could lose herself in the crowd there.

For safety she also decided to take a different cab.

Chapter 15

Next day at 1.30pm found Cecil standing at arrivals at Harry Reid Airport, formerly known as McCarran. He had a white card in his hands with the name of Abigail Frost printed on it.

Her flight from London had landed on time.

Cecil knew that it would take a little while to get through passport and immigration control, even if you were a celebrity.

US security was watertight these days in the wake of 9/11.

He had left Ricky in the limo in the parking lot.

Cecil thought that his boss was a little quiet this morning and he knew this business with the redhead woman, Angela, was slowly getting to him.

He was sure that if it wasn't for the horrific occurrences on Ruma Island, maybe Ricky wouldn't be so uptight about the latest happenings, but he could understand why his boss felt threatened. He had been through hell and back and found it hard to trust anybody fully.

Plus, America could be an unpredictable and dangerous country, where random killings occurred on a daily basis.

Being a celebrity could well put you in the firing line for some lunatic out there with a grudge or some skewed frame of mind.

Cecil knew he had to tread carefully with Ricky and just be there for him in case there was a genuine threat to his life.

* * *

Ricky sat in the passenger side of the limo with the air con on and the radio playing. He felt slightly nervous at the thought of seeing Abigail and what he had planned.

Here he was one time sex god, Ricky Wilder, now acting like a schoolboy on his first date.

He realised that he never felt like this in his previous two marriages and it dawned on him that he hadn't really known what love truly was.

Ricky could recall his drunken fights with his first wife Tracey Ann Gold. One such fight had him being chased around their Malibu home by Tracey, who was wielding a butcher knife. He had locked himself in the bathroom out of harm's way and called the police on his mobile. It had been like the scene out of the film *The Shining*.

Then there had been demure and quiet Louise Scott. An English rose and everybody's girl next door. She had been too good for him. Ricky had cheated on her more than once.

The final straw came when she arrived home to find Ricky in bed with their maid, who was only 18. The normally reasonable Louise went outside and punctured all four tyres on Ricky's beloved Ferrari, before throwing a tin of white gloss paint over the immaculate cherry red bodywork.

Happy days.

Age had mellowed Ricky, but his close brush with death had also made him appreciate each day given to him.

Now he was happy to spend his time with a woman he truly adored.

He had come a long way since his early days.

Born and raised in Lewisham, Southeast London, just six miles from Charing Cross, he came from humble beginnings. His father was a train driver and his mother a cleaner. Little did he know that when his parents finally scraped enough money together to buy him a guitar for his tenth birthday, it would set him on an incredible journey.

Both of his parents were now long gone, but not before Ricky had the chance to repay their kindness. He bought his dad a Rolls Royce and gifted both of them a villa in the Algarve.

It felt like a million miles away from his early musical days in his first band, Chameleon, with Jimmy, to his time in TNT, and finally to the mighty juggernaut that was Stormtrooper.

A lot of water and, unfortunately, blood had gone under the bridge since then.

He would like to see his days out now more peacefully.

His one big regret was never having children, but with the lifestyle he had lived, bringing a child into the world would not have been fair.

Besides, in those days, he was not ready to be a father.

As he grew older, he did think what it would have been like to have a son or a daughter or both.

Ricky had a sister, Louise, who lived in France and was four years younger than him. She had two children,

Marcus and Emily, both grown up now. When they were young, he made a point of visiting them whenever he could, cherishing the simple pleasures of playing with them and spoiling them with gifts from his travels.

The children loved having a famous uncle.

Ricky had set up a trust fund for both of them to mature when they turned 18. Although Louise had initially protested, Ricky insisted he wanted to do it. She was grateful for the good start it provided her kids, especially after losing her husband, Tony, to lung cancer at just 41, leaving her to navigate life alone.

Ricky understood all too well that you couldn't turn back the clock. Whatever regrets he had, he had to learn to live with them.

Amid the fun and glory, there had been a lot of grief and heartache. Deep down, he knew he probably wouldn't have wanted it any other way.

* * *

Suddenly, his phoned bleeped a text.

It was Cecil.

Got her with me safe and sound, boss. On our way back to the car now. Will see you in five.

Ricky found himself smiling.

His phone buzzed with another text.

This time, an unknown number appeared.

Curious, he pressed it and read the message.

Ricky, think carefully about your proposal. Angela x

Ricky stared at the message in disbelief.

He suddenly felt claustrophobic.

Ricky clamoured out of the car.

He had broken into a cold sweat.

How had this woman got his personal mobile number?

He looked around, scanning the carpark.

Was she here watching him? What the fuck did she want?

Ricky realised that he hadn't overreacted after all. This bitch was after him.

He needed to tell Joey. The police would now have to be involved. But first, he was going to have to let Abi know. She could also be in danger.

He then saw Abi on the other side of the carpark waving. Cecil was next to her, carrying her suitcase. She looked so happy and carefree.

Ricky forced a smile and waved back. He couldn't bring himself to tell her now and spoil the moment. For the time being, he decided to keep it to himself until he could speak with Joey and figure out the best way to handle it.

As Abi got closer, she ran into Ricky's arms, and they embraced, sharing a kiss.

Meanwhile, on the other side of the car park, a redhead named Angela snapped photos of the happy couple with a long-lens Nikon camera. She studied the images as they climbed into the back seat of the limo.

So, the bitch has arrived. It should be me in that backseat with Ricky. The whore has beguiled him. He can't see through her. But I can and I will do what I have to do to make Ricky see.

She watched as the limo pulled away and exited the carpark.

***

Detective Ernest Norton tucked into his twelve-inch salted beef, melted cheese and red onion sub on rye. Between mouthfuls, he sipped on a large soda.

It was his lunch break and he was sat at his cluttered desk in the Las Vegas Metropolitan Police Department situated on Joe W. Brown Drive and Paradise.

He had a heavy caseload, with the death of Eddie Bryson at the Harley Davidson Hotel and Casino as his top priority. His lieutenant had made it clear that he needed a break in the case quickly.

Ernest Norton had been on the squad 15 years and was an experienced cop. Over his time, he had seen his fair share of action on the streets. He had been shot twice, stabbed three times and glassed in the face, which resulted in the impressive scar he now sported.

Ernest had originally started his police career in New York and was on duty on 9/11 – a day that would be forever imprinted in his mind. He lost three fellow officers and good friends that day, as well as his brother-in-law, Tyrone, who served in the fire department.

Tyrone had been called to the Twin Towers amid the carnage unfolding around them. He was giving CPR to a man suffering from smoke inhalation on the pavement when he removed his own helmet to assist. In that moment, a piece of stray debris fell from the Trade Center, striking him squarely on the skull and killing him instantly. It was a terrible, freakish accident.

Life in America changed forever after that, and so did Ernest Norton. He transferred to Las Vegas three years ago when his wife, a district attorney, was offered a better position there. With four children ranging in age from 8 to 18, the decision was an easy one; they needed the stability, especially with the rising costs of family life.

The thing Ernest had to adjust to most in Vegas wasn't the completely different lifestyle but the weather. New York had seasons; Las Vegas had hot, very hot to motherfucking hot. Period.

Crime wise, both cities were pretty much the same.

Norton and his family had adapted pretty well to the change from Brooklyn East Coast to Southeastern Nevada.

Ernest Norton's partner, Maria Cortez, suddenly appeared, sipping a coffee and holding a thin manila file.

"Hey, partner. You might want to take a look at this."

With fingers sticky from ketchup and mustard, Norton spoke.

"Why don't you read it to me, Cortez? I'm in the middle of wrestling this sub into submission and I think I'm winning."

Cortez smiled.

She was a good-looking, dark-haired woman in her 30s, with classic Latina features – brown eyes and a flawless olive complexion. Behind her striking beauty was a tough cookie with a decade of street cred to her name.

She had worked with Norton since his transfer. They had pretty much hit it off from the first day they had met.

Outside of work, Ernest and his wife, Lynda, had got to know Maria, her husband Benny and their three-year-old son, Benny Jr., quite well.

Maria sat down at the desk opposite Ernest, setting down her coffee as she opened the file. She glanced at her partner, who was wolfing down another mouthful of his lunch.

"I thought Lynda had you on tuna fish and salad for lunch?"

Ernest looked up at Cortez with his mouth full and mumbled.

"Spare me the lecture and just read what you have in the file."

"I've just taken a statement from three females. They're all British and on holiday here staying at the MGM Grand. Their names are Maxine Fox, Sonia Green and Emily Bates. Maxine Fox did most of the talking. She told me a few nights ago the three of them had come back to their hotel after catching the Ricky Wilder concert at the Sunrise."

Ernest raised a hand and took a lengthy swig on his cola. He then stifled a belch and replied.

"Ricky 'Stormtrooper' Wilder is in town? How the hell did I miss that!"

Cortez seemed indifferent to the outburst.

"Who is he anyway?"

Norton looked incredulously at his partner as if she had just stepped off an alien spacecraft.

"Who is he? Who the fuck is he? He is only one of the very few genuine rock gods still alive. He's up there with Ozzy. Have you not heard of the band Stormtrooper?"

Cortez shook her head.

"Can't say I have, although I'm more of a Jennifer Lopez, Gloria Estefan girl."

Ernest shook his head.

"Carry on, Cortez."

Cortez continued.

"Apparently, they were all in the ladies' room at the MGM talking about the gig when a toilet cubicle opened, and a woman came out ranting and raving at them, claiming they knew nothing about Ricky Wilder and that she was his biggest fan. A heated argument ensued, and the woman pulled a knife from her handbag, threatening them. Thankfully, the others wisely backed off, chalking it up to crazy Vegas. Here's the punchline, Ernie: the woman with the knife was a tall redhead."

Norton stopped eating.

"Get the fuck out of here!"

Cortez nodded.

"It's true, and they provided a full description. The day after the incident, one of the women, Maxine, was checking the latest news on her phone when she saw the update on the Bryson murder, mentioning that you were still waiting for a mystery redhead to come forward in connection with it. She put two and two together and came in. That's a brief summary, but their full story is in the file."

Ernest Norton sat back in his chair, wiping his mouth and hands with a napkin. He carefully removed a spot of ketchup from his tie before placing his hands on his noticeably bulging belly.

"Okay, Cortez. Leave the file with me and I'll go through it thoroughly. We may have to go and see Mr Wilder and ask him a few questions."

"Okay, Ernie. Anything else I can do?"

"Yes, there is. Two things actually. One, bring me a black coffee, three sugars. And two, check how much the tickets are for Wilder's show, will you?"

"Maybe if you go and interview him, you might get a few freebies," said Cortez.

Norton put a scowl on his face.

"Detective Cortez, you know that would be unethical and might be construed as a bribe."

Cortez looked suitably chastised. Norton's face then split into a huge grin.

"Not a bad idea though."

Chapter 16

When Ricky returned to the hotel, he immediately brought Abigail up to his room. As soon as the door shut, they were ripping off each other's clothes in a frenzy of lust. All thoughts of the message were swept to the back of Ricky's mind.

He needed this intimacy so much right now. He wanted to feel safe in Abigail's arms.

They kissed passionately and fell onto the bed naked where they made wild, passionate love. Each of them was hungry for the other's body. It had been a while.

Once their animal urges subsided, they poured themselves some champagne, savouring the moment before making love again – this time more gently and with a sense of control. After, they both dozed off, exhausted from their exertions. Later they lazed together in the sunken tub.

"God, I've missed you, Abi," said Ricky.

Abi laughed and stretched out a long slender leg.

"I could tell. I think I need to go away more often."

Ricky grabbed her leg and began to massage the sole of her foot.

"Not for a while, eh? 'Let's get a bit of 'our' time together."

Abi took a sip of champagne.

"Don't worry, darling. I'm not going anywhere. I have two weeks pretty much free before any more work commitments."

"Great," replied Ricky, "After the show, I want to take you, the band and crew out to dinner. I've booked a table at the Eiffel Tower restaurant at the Paris."

Ricky was referring to the Paris Hotel and Casino, located midway along Las Vegas Boulevard. The hotel featured its own replica Eiffel Tower, standing an impressive 541 feet tall – about half the size of the real one in France. The renowned restaurant was located on the 11th floor, offering stunning views of the Strip.

"Sounds amazing, Ricky."

"After that, we're heading to a little club I know on Fremont Street called Queenie's. An old friend plays in the piano bar, and I would love for you to meet him. Then we can come back here for a nightcap."

"Sounds like you got it all worked out, Mr Wilder."

Ricky smiled as he now massaged her other foot.

"There's one more surprise, but you'll have to wait for that."

Abigail put her finger coyly to her lips.

"And there was I thinking I had that already."

Ricky pulled her towards him, wrapped his arms around her wet sweet-smelling body and kissed her deeply.

"The best is yet to come, my love."

* * *

Later, before Ricky's performance, they both went to the Chameleon Lounge for a drink. Ricky opted for sparkling water, focusing on his preparation for the show.

When they came into the bar, they were greeted by the glum faces of Joey, Gabriel and Cecil.

"What's up, guys?" asked Ricky, "Looks like you lost a dollar and found a dime."

Joey came over to him.

"Can I have a word in private? It won't take long."

Joey then looked at Abigail.

"Sorry to take him off you, Abi, when you've only just got here. It's work. I promise I'll have him back in a jiffy."

Abigail smiled.

"It's okay, Joey. I understand. I'll grab a drink at the bar and have a chat with Janice."

Once Abigail had moved off, Gabriel and Cecil also approached. Ricky eyed the three men and smiled nervously.

"What is it, guys? You've got me worried."

Gabriel spoke.

"It's about Jack Myers on the security desk."

Ricky looked puzzled.

"What about him?"

Gabriel sighed.

"He was found dead today in his apartment."

Ricky was shocked by the news. He had planned to speak with the man as soon as he got back on duty.

"Dead? How?"

Gabriel continued.

"Apparently, he took a tumble down the stairs and bashed his head. Became unconscious and never woke up. Police think he may have been drinking."

Ricky sat down on a sofa.

"Poor old Jack. Who would have thought? Did the police inform you?"

"Well, actually, I was in the area and thought I would call in and see him," said Gabriel, "I know he lives alone and doesn't see many people. I bought him a bottle of Wild Turkey, his favourite, and some jelly doughnuts. I rang the doorbell and knocked, but received no answer, although I could hear music from inside. Sinatra was playing. Something didn't sit right with me. After knocking again, a neighbour came out and said that the music had been playing loudly for some time and he had knocked the door earlier to complain but received no answer. He said it was out of character for Jack. I decided to call 911. Well, you know the rest…"

The assembled group were quiet for a moment. Then, Gabriel clapped his hands.

"Anyway, gentlemen, as the old saying goes, the show must go on – and it does. I'm off to make my final rounds in the Midnight Auditorium before you come down, Ricky. Also, it may seem a bit tactless, but I have cover on the security desk for Jack. Plus, Cody Wilson and his team are in the auditorium now. Lastly, Danny mentioned that the card from the newspaper had no fingerprints on it; it was clean. I've got it in my office for safekeeping. Right, I must dash."

"Thanks, Gab," replied Ricky.

Ricky looked at Joey and Cecil.

"Poor old Jack. Christ, I was only talking to him the other day and now he's gone. Fuck, people keep dying around me. Do you think I'm cursed?"

Joey rolled his eyes.

"Knock it off, Ricky. It was an accident. The old fella had one to many and took a fall. It happens."

Ricky nodded, but couldn't shake off a weird feeling about the whole thing.

* * *

Ricky stood by the curtain, ready for his entrance, with Cecil beside him. The big man was worried about his boss; he had been in this business long enough to know there were plenty of sharks lurking around.

At present, many people were poised to make a lot of money off Ricky Wilder.

Cecil was just his minder, with no agenda other than to look after his boss. That meant ensuring that no one was trying to shaft him or fuck with his karma.

"Boss…" said Cecil.

Ricky looked at the big man next to him.

"Yes?"

"I know things have been a little freaky for you the last few days, but I want you to know I have your back 100%. These other fellas can do all the security checks they want, but I'm here specifically for you. Please don't forget that."

Ricky smiled. That had been the longest speech he had ever heard Cecil make in all the time he knew him.

"Thanks, partner. I appreciate your words."

Cecil nodded and went back to staring out onto the stage as the sound crew ran their final checks.

Suddenly, Cody Wilson appeared. He was dressed all in black and sported a baseball cap and an earpiece.

"Everything is looking good, Mr Wilder And there's no sign of the mystery woman."

Ricky nodded.

"Thanks, Cody."

The security man smiled.

"I expect you hear this a million times a day, but I'm a big fan of yours and it's a privilege for me to be working for you."

"Thanks, Cody. Always good to know who your fans are."

"I know this might be a bit of a liberty, but it's my wedding anniversary tomorrow, and my wife Jen is in the audience tonight. I noticed in your set that you sing 'Lovin' You Forever' from the debut Stormtrooper album. Could I ask you to dedicate it to us? I know she would love it; it's one of her all-time favourite songs. When I first met her, I had to win her affections from you – she was obsessed with you."

Ricky always found praise uncomfortable and he felt a rush of heat race up his body.

He looked at the face of this obviously capable and hardened security professional, which at that moment resembled a little boy eagerly asking Santa Claus for a Christmas present he desperately wanted.

The song 'Lovin' You Forever' was a hugely successful ballad, often confused with the Whitesnake classic 'Is This Love'. It was a favourite at weddings and anniversary parties, a true classic among fans.

Ricky placed his hand on the man's shoulder.

"You got it, Cody. It would be my pleasure."

Cody's face broke into a relieved grin.

"People in the business were right about you," he said

"How's that?" asked Ricky.

"When I told them I was going to be working for you, they said that you were the genuine article and not a self-indulgent asshole like some other rockstars."

Ricky laughed.

"Well, I'm glad to have lived up to my reputation."

"Amen to that," chimed in Cecil.

The lights on the stage suddenly dimmed and Ricky prepared himself to go on.

"See you later, guys. Oh, and it was Jen you said was your wife's name?"

"Yes, she is sat in the third row. A blonde. She's wearing a black dress. Thanks again. She's going to be blown away."

"Go get them, boss," said Cecil.

Joey suddenly came forward.

"We good to go, Ricky?" he asked.

Ricky nodded and headed out onto the stage.

As he went on, he breathed a sigh of relief that Cody's wife Jen wasn't a redhead.

For a moment, Cody's comments had got him thinking. He was getting paranoid.

* * *

The show went off without a hitch. Ricky dedicated the song to Cody and Jen, and it was well received. Cody's wife, a stunning blonde in her 40s seated centre in the third row, was initially shocked but then beamed with joy.

Joey, Gabriel, Janice and her partner Carly, Cecil, Barry Casper, Geoff Tindel and Art Fielding all joined Ricky and Abigail at the Paris restaurant, arriving in style in a white stretch limousine.

They were escorted to a premium table by the window, perched 100 feet up, overlooking the Bellagio Hotel with its famous dancing fountains and light show across the Strip.

The food was of the highest standard, prepared by Chef Joho, known for his world-renowned French cuisine.

The entire group savoured the caviar and champagne bar before diving into their mains, which included grand seafood platters, Dover sole, Beef Wellington and roasted rack of lamb.

The fine wine flowed as they enjoyed the delicious food and engaged in lively conversation.

For dessert, they indulged in Eiffel Tower soufflés, chocolate hazelnut cake, and classic crème brûlée.

Ricky sat back, sipping a fine red Bordeaux, grateful for the weekend off. He knew his head would be pounding in the morning, but he was looking forward to a lie-in and a break from his strict routine of work and exercise.

He marvelled at the days when he was in Stormtrooper and could stay up all night drinking, do a few lines of coke or smoke weed and rise the next day with hardly any aftereffects. Oh, to be young again.

He looked around the table of friends all chatting, laughing and having a good time.

He thanked God he was alive to see this. He had been lucky and there wasn't a day that went by without him realising this.

His continued fame allowed him to dine in such opulence, but he was just as comfortable in a Denny's or Wendy's. In fact, he still loved a McDonald's sausage and egg McMuffin whenever his schedule allowed it.

He mused humorously that being a rock god was no easy task.

Ricky gazed at Abigail sitting next to him, engaged in conversation with Janice. She wore an off-the-shoulder green dress, her dark hair elegantly pinned up. Emerald earrings shimmered in the overhead lights, matching her necklace perfectly. Every so often, he caught a whiff of her Dior J'adore perfume. She looked stunning, and Ricky could hardly wait to present her with the engagement ring and ask her to be his wife.

Now seemed the perfect moment.

He picked up his glass and tapped it with his fork to get the table's attention.

"Can I have a moment of your time, please?"

The table grew quiet as everybody focused on Ricky.

"I brought you all here tonight because we're a special team and we work well together. It was my way of saying thank you. The last few years have been tough and I never envisaged ever going back on stage alone at this time of my life. Also, may I add, I never thought I would find true love at my age, but I have in the form of the gorgeous Abigail Frost."

Ricky now reached into his jacket pocket and produced a small box. He opened it and held it out towards Abi.

"Would you do me the honour of becoming my wife?"

Abigail held her hands to her cheeks in surprise and then reached for the box. She regarded the shimmering diamond engagement ring.

"Yes, I would. This is absolutely amazing. For once, I'm almost lost for words."

Ricky took the ring from the box and slipped it on her finger.

The table clapped and cheered and wished them both every success. So did people at tables in earshot.

Then, a waiter brought a large cake to the table, dripping in icing and adorned with candles and sparklers - a festive show of congratulations from the hotel.

More champagne was ordered as the night had now become extra special.

Ricky leaned in and kissed Abi gently on the lips, savouring the intoxicating aroma of her perfume.

Suddenly, his mind flashed to the scent of J'adore in his room the other day and in the empty lift. For a moment, his stomach squirmed.

This mystery woman had certainly unnerved him.

He hadn't shown anyone the text message he received at the airport. He wanted nothing to spoil this night, but he knew that tomorrow he would go to Joey, show him the message and involve the police.

It was one thing for him to be threatened, but it was not going to put Abi at risk as well. Her safety here in Vegas was paramount to him.

Ricky had resigned himself to the fact that he had to contact the police. He had his residency to finish and he couldn't go around constantly looking over his shoulder. His nerves wouldn't be able to take it.

Ricky suddenly became aware of somebody watching him. He looked across the table and met the steely gaze of Gabriel. He had never seen that look before, but just as quickly as it appeared, it vanished, replaced by a grin as Gabriel raised his wine glass in Ricky's direction.

* * *

The white stretch limousine brought everybody downtown to Fremont Street and they all walked the short distance to Queenie's. At the entrance, Gabriel seemed to hesitate, not sure whether to go in or not.

"Everything okay, Gab?" asked Ricky.

Gabriel seemed preoccupied for a moment and then he flashed his usual smile.

"Yes. All good, Ricky. I didn't realise we would be coming here."

"You know Queenie's then?" asked Ricky.

"Look at me, darling. I've lived ten years in Vegas. I'm bisexual. Of course, I know Queenie's."

The assembled group all laughed.

As they walked in, they were shown to an exclusive table near the stage and drinks were brought. Cecil, who had been drinking Pepsi all night, took his place by the table to resume his bodyguarding duties.

A few of the patrons nodded and pointed in the direction of Ricky. He was not going to remain anonymous for long, but the sheer colossal presence of Cecil would keep most fans at bay until otherwise instructed.

A female singer was just finishing off her song, a rendition of Shirley Bassey's 'Big Spender'. She was a stunning brunette with an hourglass figure poured into a shimmering silver floor-length gown.

Joey, Barry, Art and Geoff sat with their jaws wide in awe.

"Who is that?" asked a normally composed Barry, who had clearly overindulged in the vintage champagne that evening.

Gabriel leaned across the table to make himself heard.

"That's Candy," he answered.

Barry couldn't take his eyes off the woman.

"She sure is," he replied.

Gabriel laughed.

"You mean he."

Barry looked at Gabriel, tearing his eyes away from the stage.

"What do you mean, Gab?"

Gabriel chuckled.

"It is a 'he', sweety. Real name Darren Cope. He's a regular here. The club is called Queenie's because it accommodates mainly high-class drag acts."

Barry's eyes were wide.

"Are you sure?"

Gabriel looked coy.

"Yes, Barry. I'm 100% sure. I've frequented this establishment many times."

Barry shook his head.

"Well, I'll be damned. I would never have known."

"Not many would if you saw him sat at the bar."

"I always thought drag acts looked like pantomime dames. You know, Mother Goose and all that shit."

"You are so out of touch, Barry," replied Gabriel, "Most of these people are transgender. Many don't identify as a man or a woman. Las Vegas is one of the few places on earth that doesn't give a shit about your gender. It's all about entertainment."

Barry swallowed a glass of champagne.

"I'm too old for all that shit. Can't get my head around it."

"Why's that, Barry? Feeling aroused, were you?" Gabriel teased.

Barry reached for the champagne bottle

"Fuck off, Gab."

Gabriel laughed, got up and walked over to the stage as 'Candy' finished up her song. He waved and they acknowledged each other. A few seconds later, they embraced and kissed.

"Gab, honey, great to see you. It's been an age. Come backstage and meet the other girls. They'll love it that you're visiting," said Candy.

"My pleasure."

Gabriel looked back at his group.

"Excuse me, guys. Got a few old friends to say hello to. Won't be long."

They both walked off behind the curtain.

"Looks like Gabriel is at home here," commented Ricky.

"Sure does," answered Joey.

Five minutes later, from a corner stage, a piano sounded and the spotlight moved in its direction.

There was Max Sinclair, dressed in faded denims and cowboy boots, his hair tied back in its usual ponytail. He nodded to the crowd and said good evening. Then, his mellow voice started singing 'Walking in Memphis'.

Everybody sipped their drinks and listened to the magical piano and vocals. For all his flaws, the man still had class.

Thirty minutes later, during a brief interval, Max joined the table for a quick bourbon on the rocks. He embraced Ricky and Abi and shook hands with the rest of the group.

"Great set, Max," said Ricky.

"Well, thank you kindly. Glad you could all make it."

Everybody chimed in with an agreement that they loved the set.

"I will take that as a full-blown compliment coming from real music people," said Max.

He now regarded Abigail.

"So, this is your lovely lady. I've heard a lot about you, sweetheart."

Abigail smiled.

"All good, I hope."

Max looked her in the eye mischievously.

"Well, we don't want it to be all good now, do we?"

Ricky cut in.

"Yes, alright, Max. Let's keep it clean."

"Wouldn't have it any other way, Ricky. You know me."

Ricky laughed.

"Yes, I know you, so you can cut out the flirting. This lady agreed to marry me earlier this evening."

Max looked at Abigail once more.

"You sure you shouldn't be marrying a proper rockstar like Axl Rose, Dave Lee Roth or Brian Johnson?"

"I'll stick with this man, thank you," replied Abi.

Max swallowed down his drink in one gulp and stood up.

"Well, don't say I never warned you."

He blew her a kiss and bowed to the rest of the group before returning to the stage.

Halfway through the second part of his set, Max unexpectedly announced a guest singer to join him.

"Ladies and gentlemen, seated stage side tonight is the legend that is Ricky Wilder of Stormtrooper fame. I'd like to invite him to join me on stage for a duet. How about it, Ricky?"

Ricky was taken by surprise.

The crowd clapped and cheered.

Ricky looked across at his manager Joey. Joey smiled and nodded.

Ricky made his way to the stage and was handed a microphone. After a brief conversation with Max, they both sung the Rod Stewart classic 'Maggie May'.

The crowd loved it.

Ricky returned to his seat and acknowledged the crowd.

Max leaned into the mike and generously said, "Ricky has a residency up at the Sunset Hotel just off the Strip if you wish to catch his full show there."

Later after the set, everybody decided to go back to the hotel for a final nightcap.

Ricky told them that he and Abigail would have a final drink here with Max before heading back. The gang could take the limo, and he and Abi would grab a cab. Cecil said he would wait around for them, but would make sure to give them some space.

Just then, Gab, who had been backstage all that time, suddenly reappeared and took a seat next to them.

"Sorry I was so long. Had a bit of catching up to do."

"You seem to know this place well, Gab?" said Ricky.

"Yes, the place and the girls working here. I sung here a few times in the past," answered Gabriel.

"Wow, I had no idea," exclaimed Ricky.

"Why would you, Ricky? I'm only the humble stage manager. I told you there was a lot you didn't know about me."

"I didn't mean to offend you, Gab."

Gabriel held up his hand.

"I'm only teasing, dear. When I first came to Vegas, I had dreams of making it big singing. The problem was I didn't know if I wanted to sing as a boy or a girl. I did both for a while, but realised I wasn't great at either. Still, there's always some place in Vegas that will have you. Hospitality became my thing instead, although I still keep my hand in and have stepped up to the mike now and again if asked."

"You said you had sung here before?" asked Ricky.

"Yes, on a number of occasions. But then again, I 've played most of the clubs in downtown at one time or another."

"You must know Max then as he's been here some years," said Ricky.

"Only by sight. Usually when I'd done my turn here, I was hurrying on my way to another club to sing. You didn't get much time to socialise."

Gabriel spied Max Sinclair making his way through the crowd towards the table.

He got up rather hurriedly.

"Anyway, I will love you and leave you. I'm off to have a drink with the 'girls' for old times' sake. Both of you enjoy the rest of the evening and congratulations once more."

He then looked at Abi.

"I hope you realise what a prince you have got there, my dear."

With that, he headed for the exit.

Abigail excused herself and made her way to the restroom.

Max ordered a round of drinks from the cocktail waitress and joined Ricky.

"Who was the fella just leaving?" he asked.

"That's Gabriel Hart. The manager of the Midnight Auditorium at the Sunset," answered Ricky, "Why do you ask?"

Max took a seat.

"Just looked familiar. That's all."

"Apparently, he used to sing here now and again," answered Ricky.

"That could be it," mused Max, "Anyway, did you enjoy the show?"

"Great set, Max. You seem happy here."

"Yeah. It's a pretty cool place and pretty much trouble free. The people that come in here are gentle souls," replied Max, "Some of the dives I played, you risked your life just going out on stage. This suits me fine. The clientele are mostly LGBTQ. It takes all sorts to make the world go around and I don't judge. Fuck it, we are in Vegas, for Christ's sake. The place is popular. We've had a few impromptu performances over the years from some big-name singers. Let me show you this."

Max gestured to the back wall and they all got up and walked to it. The wall was plastered with photographs, ranging from the present to way back.

Ricky studied them. Max was right about the star singers. He picked out Barry Manilow, Johnny Mathis, Dusty Springfield, K.D. Lang and Sam Smith.

"Quite a who's who," commented Ricky.

His attention was then drawn to photos of the drag acts that played in the club.

"Those were famous drag singers over the years. Tricia, Kylie, Roseanne, Gloria. Great acts. Class."

As he took a closer look at the photos, his blood suddenly ran cold. Staring back at him was the redhead. It was a close-up of her smiling at the camera. Ricky had no doubt it was her.

Max leaned in.

"Wouldn't know that they were not female, would you?"

Ricky pointed to the photograph.

"Do you know who that is there?"

"She's a beauty, eh? I feel strange saying that about a man, but she's a hell of a lot more attractive than some of the women I've taken to bed in the past."

Ricky was gobsmacked. The mystery woman was really a man. This had now thrown a curve ball his way.

"Her name, I recall, is Angela. She has been part of the singing act here in downtown on and off for some years," continued Max

"Does she still come in here?" asked Ricky.

"Haven't seen her for a while. Mind you, I haven't seen what she looks like out of her frock, so to speak. I don't know her male persona. They could be sat at the bar now and I would never know. They like to keep their identities secret. Excuse me, Ricky. I need the little boys' room. Fucking old age has me pissing like a pony these days."

Ricky took out his mobile phone and snapped a photo of the smiling Angela. He then went back to his seat and made short work of the Jack Daniel's that Max had ordered him.

"Are you okay?" You've gone awfully quiet," Abi was back.

Ricky smiled weakly at her.

"Sorry, love. I've just come over a little tired. Must be the occasion."

Abi leaned in and squeezed his thigh.

"Not too tired, I hope."

Ricky laughed.

"We will have one for the road and then get out of here. How's that sound?"

"Like music to my ears," replied Abigail

Outside the club, Max waited with Ricky while Cecil phoned the Sunset to send a cab down to collect them. As Abigail chatted with Cecil, Ricky seized the opportunity to speak to Max.

"Max, do me a favour. This Angela character, can you ask around and see if anybody knows who they really are outside their singing persona?" asked Ricky.

"What's the sudden interest in the drag act? Something you need to tell me, Ricky?" answered Max.

"Very funny. No, I'm just curious as I think this person could be staying at the Sunset Hotel and they appear to have an unhealthy interest in me."

"Do you care to enlarge on that statement?" asked Max.

Ricky looked in Abigail's direction.

"Not the time and place, my friend. Can you just help me out here and trust me? I will fill you in later."

"Well, I'll give it a shot, but like I said, most of these acts keep their true identities to themselves. You rarely see them out of their make-up and costumes. If you did, unless they told you who their stage persona was, you'd be none the wiser. Sometimes, I think even they don't know who the hell they are."

Ricky saw Abigail heading towards them.

"Just see what you can do, Max."

Max nodded.

"Well, thanks again for coming down," he added, hugging both Ricky and Abigail.

"Look after yourself, Max. We'll speak soon. Goodnight," said Ricky.

The cab pulled up and Cecil opened the back doors for his boss and Abigail. He jumped in the front with the driver and looked back over his shoulder.

"Back home?" he asked.

Ricky nodded.

"Yes, please."

The cab pulled away from the curb into the night.

Chapter 17

Max lit a cigar as he watched the cab disappear, reflecting on what a good night it had been. It was always a pleasure to see his old buddy, Ricky.

He cherished the times he travelled with Stormtrooper and the many gigs he had been a part of, with Japan being his favourite tour. What a place, and what a culture! He often thought about packing up and heading out there for an extended vacation – or maybe even longer. Perhaps one day. But he knew deep down that he needed to kick the booze before that dream could become a reality.

Maybe next year.

Max breathed in the warm night air and walked around the side of the club to an alleyway, hoping to finish his cigar in peace before heading home – or maybe he would have just one more for the road, though he couldn't quite remember how many he had already had. He knew the sensible thing would be to leave, but the lure of the bottle was too strong.

Home was a small apartment a few blocks away. Nothing special, but now that he was on his own, it suited his purposes. It felt empty, so why rush back? Only the cat would be there to keep him company, and it only showed up when it was hungry.

Cats were selfish bastards. The worst sort of pet to own. They answered to nobody and didn't give a shit.

Max mused that he had known many people exactly like that as well.

Suddenly, a voice spoke from the darkness startled him.

"You recognised me inside the club, didn't you, Max? Did you tell Ricky who I was?"

Max glazed into the darkness.

"Who is it?" he asked.

A man walked forward, someone Max had seen earlier in the evening. Once again, his face looked familiar, but Max couldn't quite place him.

"Sorry, mister. You have the wrong guy. I don't know you," continued Max.

The man smiled, his pearly white teeth shining in the gloom.

"You know me as Angela. The red-haired drag act. You were showing Ricky Wilder my photo on the club wall."

The penny then dropped.

"You're Angela? Well, I'll be damned. I would never have known. I don't recall your real name, and certainly Ricky doesn't know, although he did express an interest in you. I told him I didn't know you outside of your act, but he did ask me to try and find out. He seemed very interested in you."

The man stepped closer.

"Well, now you know, Max, but I can't take that chance that you won't blab straight to Ricky, even if I ask you not to," he said.

Max could now see the man more clearly and, in that moment, he did recall who he was. He was the man sat with Ricky earlier that evening.

"Wait a moment. You're that guy from the Sunset Hotel. Ricky said you were the entertainments manager. I don't understand what's going on here..."

Max didn't see the knife until it pierced his abdomen. His reflexes were dulled from too much alcohol, and he staggered back in surprise, hitting the wall.

"I can't have you telling Ricky who I am, Max. I'm sorry, old timer. Things are at a crucial stage, you see."

Before Max could respond, the knife went in again.

The older man slumped to the floor.

The other man looked up and down the street, then bent over Max's body to check his carotid pulse. There was none. Satisfied he had done his job properly, he tossed the knife into a nearby storm drain and walked away unnoticed.

His secret was still safe for now.

* * *

Ricky awoke the next morning and immediately took a shower. After, he brewed some coffee and rummaged through his washbag for paracetamol, as he had a pounding headache.

He took two tablets with a large glass of water.

Once the coffee was ready, he poured two cups and brought them to the bedside.

He leaned over and kissed Abigail gently on the lips. She awoke and cuddled him.

"Morning, you. How do you feel?" she asked

"Rather fragile after last night's festivities."

"And there I was thinking I was marrying a hellraising rock god."

"I think I've raised enough hell to last a lifetime. I feel like shit."

Abigail laughed.

"Well, you did give the champagne and red wine a hammering, sweetheart."

Ricky slid back into bed and sipped his coffee.

"That I did, but it was all worth it. Are you happy?"

Abigail sat up and reached for him, kissing once again.

"Never happier, Ricky," she answered as she regarded her ring.

Ricky took another sip of coffee. Damn, it tasted good.

"Listen, Abi. I need to tell you something. I didn't want to spoil last night, so I let it wait, but now I need to put you in the picture."

Abigail sensed the seriousness in Ricky's voice.

"What is it, Ricky? You're scaring me."

Ricky went on to spill the whole story of the mystery redhead right up to the phone text. Abigail listened intensely and said nothing until he had finished.

"Christ, Ricky. This person sounds unstable and also a possible killer. You should have already informed the police."

"I know, Abi, but Joey and Gab told me I was more or less overreacting."

"It's not their ass on the line here, Ricky. It's you in the firing line again if this woman comes looking for you. You've been through enough."

"I realise that now. Plus, I'm also concerned for your safety."

"My safety. Why?" asked Abigail.

"Whoever this person is, they don't seem too happy that I was going to propose to you. They have this warped logic that they believe they can be with me and nobody else. I think they won't stop at anything to try and achieve that, including hurting you."

Abigail felt a shiver run up her spine and she pulled herself closer to Ricky.

"Hold me, darling."

Rick held her tight and stroked her hair.

"Once we're dressed, I'll find Joey and let him know that we want the police involved."

***

Detectives Ernest Norton and Maria Cortez stood in Gabriel Hart's office. Gab phoned upstairs to let Ricky know the police were here.

Earlier, Ricky had shown Joey the text message and the photo image. For the first time, Joey began to show real concern. This escalated when Janice had shown them Ricky's Facebook and Instagram pages. They had been hacked into and were littered with one repeated message from an unknown person just calling themselves 'The Scarlet Witch'.

The message read:

I told you not to propose to the bitch. Now you will pay.

This was the final nail in the coffin.

Nobody outside the group at the meal the previous evening knew about his proposal, so it had to be someone close to home who let the information slip. This suggested that they knew the redhead.

This all added up to warrant the phone call to the police department.

When Detective Norton received the call from Joey Bruce, he could hardly believe it. He was just getting ready to come visit Ricky Wilder at the Sunset on the back of the incident the three British women had incurred in a restroom at the MGM.

Grabbing his jacket from the back of his chair, he called out to Maria Cortez as he made his way out to the squad car.

* * *

Gabriel smiled at the officers and gestured to one of the sofas.

"Please take a seat. Ricky won't be a minute. Would you like tea? Coffee? Water?"

Both officers settled on the sofa, but declined a drink.

A knock on the door had Gab call out to come in.

Joey and Ricky entered.

Abigail had opted to stay with Janice and let Ricky get on with things.

Norton and Cortez both stood and produced their shields.

"Detective Norton and Cortez. Las Vegas Police Department."

Joey nodded.

"I'm Joey Bruce, the one you spoke to on the phone, and this is Ricky Wilder."

They all shook hands and then sat down on the various sofas and chairs.

For a second, Ernest Norton had to focus on his job. He was a little in awe. Here he was, sitting but a few feet away from one of the greatest rockstars of his generation. A solid gold legend. He had every record released by Stormtrooper and Wilder.

Maria Cortez coughed and discreetly dug her elbow into Norton's rib. This brought him back to the present.

"Mr Wilder, in your own time, tell me your story from the start about this red-headed woman."

"Please call me Ricky. I hate formality."

Norton nodded.

"Okay, Ricky. Carry on."

Ricky explained everything: the rose and card left outside his room, the unsettling feeling that someone had been in his space on more than one occasion, the missing t-shirt and the fleeting glimpses of a red-haired woman in the hotel. He recounted seeing her one night in the audience and finding the card tucked inside the newspaper. He mentioned his conversation with cab driver Dwight Fielding, the news of the death at the Harley Davidson club, the threatening text messages and the concerning posts on his social media pages. He also showed the detectives the photo he had taken in Queenie's, which he had sent to both their phones. By the time he finished presenting everything, the evidence seemed pretty damning to everyone in the room.

"You have no idea at all who this woman is?" asked Norton.

"Up to last night, I wasn't even sure that she existed. I take it you know about my experience on Ruma Island and the murders?"

Both detectives nodded in the affirmative.

Ricky continued.

"I wasn't sure if it was some sort of delayed shock. That was why I was reluctant to involve you and waste your time."

"What has changed your opinion now?" asked Cortez.

"Well, apart from the messages last night, I was at a club downtown called Queenie's. A friend of mine, Max Sinclair, performs in the piano bar there. He showed me photographs of the stars who have played there, along with pictures of the drag acts that have performed on the main stage in cabaret. One photo immediately caught my eye – the redhead named Angela. I'm 99% sure she's the mystery woman. I got a good look at her in the audience, and she looked the same. Plus, the names match. Also, nobody outside my group last night knew about my proposal to Abi. To me, that means someone close to home is leaking information."

Norton was scribbling down notes as Ricky spoke.

"Did your friend Max know who this Angela really was?"

Ricky shook his head.

"No. But he was going to look into it for me."

Norton looked around the room.

"Does anybody else know who this Angela may be?"

Ricky looked towards Gabriel.

"You said you had sung there at the club a few times, Gab?"

Gabriel looked a little flustered.

"I have, love, but a lot of acts come and go. I have no recollection of anybody named Angela. From the photo you showed me, she's very striking. I wouldn't have forgotten if I met her."

He then pulled his phone from his jacket pocket and checked it.

"Sorry, I'm needed at the auditorium. Can I go, Detective?"

Norton nodded.

"Yes. Thank you, Mr Hart. We will be in touch if we need to speak to you again."

Gabriel headed for the door.

"See you all later," he said as he left the room.

Norton got up from the sofa.

"I'm going to head down to Queenie's and ask around. I'll get some of my colleagues to do the same in other clubs downtown. We'll pass the image around – somebody must know who this is. One problem we face is that the drag act circles can be pretty secretive and tend to close ranks. We might have a hard time getting people to talk," said Norton, "Detective Cortez will stay here and speak with all who were present at your dinner celebrations last night. I will keep you up to speed with any updates. As long as your security is tight, carry on with your schedule, but try not to be left alone in public."

Joey spoke up.

"We are okay for the shows to continue then?"

"As long as you have security present, then I think they'll be fine. Plus, selfishly, I would like to get up here to see it myself if possible."

Joey smiled.

"I'm sure a couple of tickets could be arranged."

"Well, I'll be in touch as soon as I've been downtown. Don't worry, Ricky. Now this is all out in the open, we will find this Angela, especially as she still seems to be around."

Everybody shook hands.

"Let me show you out," offered Joey.

Just then, Detective Cortez's phone rang.

"Excuse me," she said as she answered it.

A moment later, she cut the call, took Norton to one side of the room and spoke privately to him.

Eventually, he turned back to the room.

"Ricky, you mentioned a friend… Max Sinclair."

"Yes, that's right. Max and I go back a long way. Why do you ask?"

"I'm afraid I have some bad news. Mr Sinclair's body was found earlier this morning in an alley at the side of Queenie's club. He had been stabbed to death."

Ricky suddenly felt the room spinning and collapsed back onto the sofa.

Chapter 18

Ricky woke up on his bed. Abigail was sat in a chair close to him reading. She saw him sit up.

"How the hell did I get here?"

Abigail put her book down.

"You passed out in Gab's office. When you came to, the hotel doctor checked you over and administered a sedative to let you sleep and get over the shock. Cecil was then summoned and he threw you over his shoulder like a ragdoll and brought you up here."

Ricky ran his hands through his hair.

"How long have I been asleep?"

Abigail looked at her wristwatch.

"Just over three hours."

"Shit. I can't get my head around poor old Max. What was it? A mugging?"

Abigail shook her head.

"According to Detective Cortez, apparently not. The body still had a wallet, phone and wristwatch on it. There were also no defensive wounds on his hands. Whoever did this murdered him in cold blood."

Just like the man in the Harley D bar.

Ricky hung his head in sorrow.

"Why? Max wouldn't hurt a fly. He had no enemies I know of. Who would do this?"

Ricky got out of bed.

"I need a drink."

He headed to the room bar.

"Do you think that is wise with the medication you've taken?" said Abigail with concern in her voice.

"Fuck it," replied Ricky and poured himself a large measure of bourbon, downing it in two gulps. He started filling the tumbler again.

Abigail came up to him.

"Ricky, I'm truly sorry for what happened to your friend, but your grief will not stop by hitting the bottle, nor will it bring him back."

Ricky stopped pouring and put the bottle down. He pulled Abigail close to him and held her like his whole life depended on it.

"Why do the people I love and hold dear to me keep dying? I don't think I can take much more pain. The thought of losing you terrifies me."

Tears came to his eyes and he wept.

Abigail said nothing, but just held him and stroked his head. She persuaded him to go back to bed and rest.

There was nothing they could do at the moment, but wait and see what the police could come up with.

* * *

Detective Ernest Norton spoke to Wesley Bauer, the manager of Queenie's. Other police were interviewing the staff who were on duty last night.

"I don't know what to tell you, Detective. I didn't see or hear anything out of the ordinary. Max did his slot as usual and I did see him go outside with that Ricky Wilder guy. I went back up to my office and presumed that Max had gone off with Wilder to party somewhere.

The first I knew about Max was when one of my cleaners went around to the alleyway with some garbage bags and found the body. Then, I phoned you guys. There is no CCTV in that alley. I wish to Christ I could tell you more. Max was more than just an employee; he was a friend."

Norton nodded and regarded the wall of photos. He spotted the redhead instantly and pointed.

"Mr Bauer, do you know who that is?"

Bauer looked at the photograph.

"Sure. It's a drag act named Angela. She used to do a few stints here going back a while."

"Do you know the person behind the drag act?"

Bauer smiled ruefully.

"These acts come in through the back of the club, head straight to their dressing rooms and get made up. I rarely see them out of make-up. They could be anyone."

Norton inwardly cursed. He half guessed already this would be the case.

"Would anybody else have an idea? The other girls in the photo, do any of them still work here?"

Bauer studied the photograph again.

"Yeah, one there on the right, Candy. She performed last night."

"She here now?"

"No. She won't be back until Monday."

"You have an address for her?" asked Norton.

"Give me a few moments and I'll check my files in the office. Anybody currently on our books, I keep a contact address and number for. Before you ask, I wouldn't have kept any record of Angela. It must be well over a year since she performed here."

Norton went to the bar and ordered a Coke. He was given it on the house by the barman.

Norton studied the photo wall again and saw some famous faces staring back at him.

He loved his music and had an eclectic taste ranging from Marvin Gaye to Elton John to David Bowie to Stormtrooper and Zeppelin.

He thought about Ricky Wilder. That man had been through a lot and somehow survived, but it had obviously left its mark on him.

By finding this mystery woman and being able to exclude her from any hint of murder or foul play would go a long way to easing Wilder's fears.

A stalking fan was one thing, a killer was another.

Ricky Wilder had seen enough death and destruction to last a lifetime. He deserved closure. Yet in the world of high celebrity, you were always vulnerable to the weirdos and creeps that might target you. Maybe that is the price you pay for fortune and fame.

Suddenly, Wesley Bauer appeared with a piece of paper in his hand.

"Here we go, Detective. One address for Miss Candy Caine, aka Darren Cope."

Norton took the proffered paper and studied the address. Candy lived at the Pinetree Apartments at the junction of East Carson Ave and Third Street. It was only about five minutes from here.

Ernest Norton thanked Wesley Bauer and left the club.

He walked to his car and jumped in, calling Cortez to update her on where he was headed. She informed him that she had spoken to everyone in the Wilder party from last night, and they all appeared clean. He told

Cortez that if she was ready to wrap things up and head back to the station, he would call in after visiting Candy Caine.

Pinetree Apartments were easy enough to find. The building could do with a lick of paint; otherwise, it looked presentable.

Norton was looking for number 21 on the second floor and was pleasantly surprised to find the elevator working.

Most tourists wouldn't see the seedier and more downtrodden side of the city. For most, Las Vegas was the Strip and Fremont Street. They didn't know the underbelly of the place and why should they?

Some parts of downtown should not be visited by tourists or out of towners. They were too dangerous. This part of Vegas, where the Pinetree Apartments were, was one such place.

Norton found the apartment and knocked on the door. A moment later, the door was opened by a white male around 28. He was blonde and stood around 6 feet. He eyed the bulky figure of the man outside.

"Yes?" the younger man asked.

Norton showed his ID.

"Darren Cope?"

The man looked puzzled.

"Yes. What can I do for you?"

"I wonder if it's possible to have a word. Did you know about the murder outside Queenie's last night?"

The man paled and held onto the door jamb.

"Murder. What murder? Who?"

"May I come in to speak to you?" said Norton.

Cope stepped aside and let the Detective in saying, "Go straight on down the passage to the living area."

Norton came into a light and airy lounge/kitchen area. It was brightly painted and flamboyantly furnished.

"Please sit down."

Norton sat into a plush leather recliner.

"You mentioned murder, Detective,' said Cope as he sat on the sofa and curled his bare feet under himself. Norton noticed his toenails had bright pink polish on them, which matched his fingernails.

"The resident singer, Max Sinclair, was knifed to death in the side alley of the club sometime around 2.00am."

Darren Cope looked genuinely shocked.

"Oh Christ, no. Not Max. He was a sweetheart. Do you know who did this?"

Norton shook his head.

"This is what we're trying to find out and I need your help."

Cope looked up and suddenly clutched his throat.

"Dear God, you don't suspect me, do you? I wouldn't hurt a fly, and Max was a friend."

Norton held up a hand.

"No, Mr Cope. That's not why I'm here. I've spoken with Wesley Bauer earlier on and he told me you left the club around 1.30am with friends. You are not a suspect."

This seemed to pacify the younger man.

"So, how can I help?"

Norton showed him the image on his phone.

"Do you know who this is?"

Cope studied the photo.

"Yes, it's Angela. She used to sing at Queenie's a while ago. We became friends, then she suddenly left. She left singing and got another job. You know what

Vegas is like: one minute you're flavour of the month, the next you're on the scrapheap."

"Have you seen her recently?" asked Norton.

"Well, here's the strangest thing. I hadn't until last night and then she walked into the club out of the blue."

Norton suddenly leant forward in his chair. A tingle of adrenaline coursed through his stomach.

"Go on," he urged.

"Well, it wasn't really Angela, but her alter ego. You know, the manly side of her. She came backstage for a while to meet some of the other girls and then we arranged to go for a drink after. We were going to Binion's Casino for a cocktail and a little flutter when she said she'd left her mobile phone back in the restrooms at Queenie's. She told us all to go on to the casino and she would catch us up."

"And did she?" asked Norton.

"Yes, about 30 minutes later, she joined us," replied Cope.

Norton felt a sweat come to his brow as he asked the next question.

"Mr Cope, do you know Angela's male name?"

"Yes, it's Gabriel. Like the angel. Gabriel Hart."

Norton instantly knew that he had recently heard the name. Then, it came to him.

Gabriel Hart. The entertainments manager of the Sunset Casino and Hotel. The man whose office he had been in early that morning. A man very close to Ricky. A man who had his complete trust. Was he truly the redhead who had been stalking him?

"Is Gabriel in trouble, Detective?" said Cope with fear in his voice.

"That, I don't know, but I need to speak to him urgently."

"I can't believe Gabriel would murder anybody."

"Well, Mr Cope, as you well know from your chosen profession, everybody can have another side to their personality. Some have many," said Norton, "But he can get help if I find him."

Darren Cope took this on board and then spoke.

"I don't know if this helps, but while Gab was singing in downtown, he rented an apartment a few blocks from here at a complex called the Oasis. It was a ground floor flat, number 4. I went there are few times for a short while we were lovers," said Cope, "The thing with Gab was that he was never quite sure who he was. It felt as if he was constantly battling between his male and female sides, each jostling for superiority. He also had a temper that he often found hard to control."

"You think he's schizophrenic?" enquired Norton.

"I'm no doctor, Detective. Let's say he was highly strung, to say the least," replied Cope.

Norton smiled and changed tact.

"You think he might still rent this apartment?"

"It might be worth a try."

As an afterthought, Cope added, "I hope to God he isn't the person you're after."

Norton pulled out his phone and dialled Maria Cortez. She answered almost instantly.

Norton filled her in on the latest developments and where he was heading. He also told her of his suspicions about Hart.

"See if you can find him and just keep an eye on him until I get back. I don't want to cause a scene or spook him until I'm sure what we're dealing with."

He closed the call.

Norton thanked Darren Cope and left. Ten minutes later, he stood outside flat number 4 at the Oasis. He checked his gun and put it back in his holster. Knocking on the door, he waited.

There was no sound or movement from inside the apartment. Another five minutes of knocking convinced him that nobody was at home.

Norton found the janitor of the building, a man named Oscar who looked a hundred years old. He showed his ID and explained that he needed to get into apartment number 4 quickly.

Oscar handed him a spare key and mentioned that, to his knowledge, it was still being rented, though he wasn't sure by whom. He thought it might be a woman.

* * *

Norton opened the door and shouted, "Anybody at home? Police."

He drew his gun and wished he had called for backup. Too late now.

Anyway, this could prove to turn out a dead end.

It didn't take Norton long to search the main rooms of the apartment. The place was clean and tidy. He wasn't sure one way or the other that somebody was living here on a regular basis.

There were no odours of cooking in the air, and the bathroom was clean. The kitchen cupboards were empty, as were the sink and draining board. No half-squeezed tubes of toothpaste or partially used shower gel anywhere on view.

The shower stall was dry. The bathroom cabinet was bare, except for a lone pill bottle. The label was faded, but he could read the word Diazepam on it. He put the bottle back.

He now moved into a spacious bedroom. The bed was made up and the room was tidy. The apartments décor was neutral, as were the furnishings. There seemed nothing of a personal nature displayed. All this combined made it hard to ascertain whether it was a male or female who lived here.

Walking around the bed, Norton moved to the other side of the room. A large built-in wardrobe covered the far wall. Norton tried the doors, but they were locked. He looked nearby for keys, but could not locate any. Reaching in his jacket pocket, he produced a small lock knife. He worked the blade into the lock and managed to open it quite quickly.

Norton opened both doors to reveal a deceptively large walk-in space adorned with glamorous dresses, shoes and wigs. Beyond the clothes was a dressing table with make-up, perfumes and other cosmetics on top. A large, gilded mirror was on the wall above it.

This was totally unexpected. It was like a backstage dressing room of a theatre.

He studied the wigs. There were all sorts of colours there and there were four red ones. This sparked his interest. He had a feeling that he was on the right trail.

He now moved out of the master bedroom and walked down the hall to another closed door, which looked like a spare bedroom. Norton found the door locked, but again, made short work of opening it.

The room was dark due to the curtains being drawn.

Walking briskly across the room, the policeman pulled open the curtains, letting daylight flood in. He turned and gasped as he took in the far wall, which was covered in photographs, newspaper articles, and magazine clippings – all dedicated to Ricky Wilder.

Getting closer, Norton studied the wall and saw articles charting Wilder throughout his career right up to the Ruma Island murders, his residency here in Las Vegas and his blossoming relationship with actor Abigail Frost.

The wall was like a shrine to the rockstar.

The thing that disturbed Norton most was a picture of Abgail Frost that had been taken recently. In red marker pen written across the image were the words:

Die, bitch.

Bingo. He had struck gold.

Norton reached for his phone. He needed to let Cortez know what he had discovered.

Suddenly, a floorboard creaked behind him. Before he could react, a strong arm wrapped around his neck and squeezed in a vicelike grip. A voice now whispered close to his ear.

"This is a carotid stranglehold. I am slowing the blood flow to your brain by closing down the carotid arteries running up each side of your neck. It's an incredibly clever technique. Once on properly, it doesn't matter how big you are, you're going to sleep in five to fifteen seconds."

Norton couldn't argue with that as black dots appeared in front of his eyes.

The voice continued.

"If held on for three minutes or more, the brain will die. It can be a killing technique. But a quicker method still is the chokehold against the windpipe crushing the larynx."

The arm changed position so the forearm was directly against the windpipe. Norton began to gag as his airway was shut down.

"A really nasty way to go. Oh, Detective. You really shouldn't have found this place. I hate what I have to do to you, but you've left me no choice. As I told Max Sinclair before he died, I can't reveal myself just yet. Thank God, good old Darren rang me and put me in the picture. I couldn't have you telling anybody else now, could I? Maybe you already did… either way, you must die."

Norton gave up his struggle and slowly sank to the carpet. Looking down at him was a triumphant looking Gabriel Hart.

* * *

Gabriel walked into the wardrobe in the bedroom. He wasn't surprised to find the doors open. Detective Norton had certainly got the full tour. Nosey fucker.

He lifted a long red wig and placed it over his short blonde hair. Moving to the mirror, he admired himself.

He was instantly Angela. Gabriel was fading into the background.

It had always been like this on and off for as long as he could recall, but the urge to be Angela was getting stronger day by day.

But Angela was a bad girl. A dangerous girl.

Gabriel had always struggled with his sexuality, cruising between male and female. He had been happy flitting from Gabriel to Angela whenever the mood suited him, especially in his drag act. But outside of that, they had shared completely separate lives.

His mother had first caught him dressing up in her clothes and wearing her make-up when he was 14 years old. She was shocked, but told him that she wouldn't tell his father if he promised not to do it again.

Gabriel promised, but he knew it was a lie. He couldn't stop himself. He didn't want to.

He chose the name Angela after a teacher he had a crush on in high school—Miss Weiss, who taught music.

She was an extremely attractive redhead, and Gabriel had been smitten with her. He loved everything about her. Her dress sense, hair, smile, laugh, wit, intelligence, self-confidence, poise and her musical skills. She had a voice like an angel when she sang.

He wanted to be her.

When she left Iowa for New Jersey, Gabriel was gutted, but he never forgot her.

As a young man, Gabriel had a few girlfriends, but they never understood him and thought he was a weirdo or creep, especially Gloria Reed.

He had confided in her his secret desires and she encouraged him to dress up for her. When he did, she took photos of him as Angela and then told him that she was going to spread them around school.

She tried to blackmail him for money. He paid her the initial $100 she asked for, but she came back for more.

Gabriel knew she would keep coming back, so instead of paying Gloria, he strangled her and drove her out into the cornfields and buried her body. It was never found.

Later, a lover named Felix Hardy had also found out about Gabriel when he had arrived home early from work to the apartment they shared at the time. He found Gabriel dressed and made-up as Angela and was appalled.

Felix began to pack his bags and told Gabriel that he was going to tell all their friends. Again, Gabriel couldn't allow this, so Felix went missing and has never been found.

From then on, he kept his dual life a secret.

Eventually, he left for Las Vegas to find like-minded people.

Gabriel wasn't really effeminate. He was a tough cookie that could look after himself, with a passion for fitness and martial arts. His fitness and diet made sure that he had the sort of figure and curves that would pour into a dress convincingly. He waxed and shaved his body daily to maintain his feminine side. Yes, he could be flamboyant, sometimes even camp, but he never flaunted his sexuality in anybody's face.

In recent times, Angela had become increasingly dominant due to her obsession with Ricky Wilder. It was even worse, as Gabriel saw Ricky every day and was close to him, sharing meals, conversations and attending to his every need.

To keep in the persona of Gabriel Hart, entertainments manager, was now a struggle.

Angela had got him to do bad things like drop gifts at Ricky's room or enter it and tamper with stuff.

Security guard old Jack Myers had genuinely been diagnosed with Alzheimer's, but every now and then, he had been able to recall things and he remembered Gabriel bringing a gift of a rose down to Ricky Wilder's room.

Gabriel had tried to convince Jack that he was imagining it, so Jack went to look it up on the security footage. That was when Gabriel beat him to it and deleted it.

After this, Gabriel knew that Jack Myers was a liability as he kept telling Gabriel that he was convinced that he had seen him deliver the rose. When Ricky had told Gabriel he was going to speak to Jack, he couldn't let that happen. So, Angela had persuaded him to pay Jack a visit at his apartment and push him down the stairs to his death.

Stealing Ricky's vest had been a spur of the moment thing by Angela herself after arriving back from nightclubbing to the Sunrise Hotel. She had entered the hotel through the basement, passed the swimming pool by chance and saw Ricky in the water. On impulse, she took the disregarded vest. Risky but exciting.

Angela was obsessed with Ricky, so much so that if anybody badmouthed him or thought they knew him better than her, they would pay the price. Like the loud-mouthed drunk in the Harley. The three bitches in the MGM restrooms had been lucky. Max Sinclair had been collateral damage, as would be Darren Cope.

Gabriel wanted to dress up now. Angela was desperate to materialise, but he fought the urge hard. He had work to complete.

He also needed to keep this place secret. It was his haven and he returned here many a night when he couldn't risk going back as Angela to the Sunrise. Angela was now dominant, but she knew she would have to stay in her alter ego of Gabriel for now to make her plan work.

Angela hated Gabriel. He was too emotional and too fucking soft. This made him weak, not like her.

She was safe again for now. She rationalised that all the police had was circumstantial evidence. Could they be 100% sure that she was the redhead? Could they recognise that it was Gabriel Hart?

Doubtful on both counts.

Gabriel had always been careful with who he shared his alter ego with, whether they knew him as a male or female. He tried to keep the two separate because usually they were.

Until now.

Of course, Darren Cope, aka Candy, knew who he was due to their brief relationship.

That would be okay, though, because Gabriel was on his way now to Darren's apartment to thank him for the tipoff and silence him forever. Poor sucker. As soon as he had made that phone call to Gabriel, he was a dead man.

The policeman was out of the picture, so was that Max character at Queenie's. He knew it was risky going in the club last night, but he had no idea Ricky was taking everybody there until they pulled up outside. He could hardly have run off. That would have drawn suspicion.

So, he had decided to go backstage to avoid Max Sinclair. They had shared a late nightcap at the club about a year ago after both performing there. They got drunk and talked for a while, but Gabriel knew it would only be a matter of time before Max made the connection between him and Angela.

He had to go.

Now it was the turn of that bitch Abigail.

How dare she steal Ricky away from Angela when she had been so devoted to him for years. It just wasn't fair.

Get her out of the picture and the playing field would be free for Angela once more. She would finally expose her love for him.

Yes, he would be distraught for a while in losing Abigail, but she would help him get over it. After all, she was his biggest fan and the only one who really understood him.

She knew everything about him, from his childhood to the superstar he was now. She understood him better than that woman, Abigail. With time, Ricky would come to realise this fact. He had to.

What if he didn't play ball?

At this moment, Gabriel did not want to contemplate the alternative.

Chapter 19

Detective Maria Cortez had gone down to the auditorium where Gabriel Hart had said he was heading, but there was no sign of him. Some technicians were working in there, but they all confirmed that they didn't know where he was and hadn't seen him recently.

After an hour of searching and asking staff, she concluded that he had left the hotel. This was confirmed when she found his red Corvette was missing from his parking spot.

Cortez pondered on whether to put a call out to traffic to look for the car. She decided to phone Norton to see what he thought. The call went to answerphone.

Five minutes later, she tried again with the same result.

After trying twice more with no luck, Cortez got a growing sense of unease rising in her body.

She thought Norton would have contacted her before now and she was concerned that he wasn't answering her calls. She decided to drive downtown to the address Norton had given her earlier and check things out.

Cortez left an officer at the hotel with the strict instructions to contact her if Gabriel Hart returned. As she started up her car, she had a bad feeling about the situation.

* * *

Gabriel pulled into his parking space just as Cortez left. He saw her go and deduced that she was probably heading downtown.

Time was running out, as the bodies of the big cop and Candy would soon be discovered. Cortez would have seen the apartment and would eventually put the pieces together.

He had been fond of Darren and had tried to make his death by strangulation as painless as possible. Darren hadn't put up much resistance, and his neck was weak. He died quickly.

Now, he needed to find Abigail Frost and dispose of her. Then the path would be clear for him and Ricky.

Ideally, he planned to separate Abigail from Ricky and dispose of her, but now he didn't have the time.

Things hadn't gone as she had planned and there had been too many deaths.

He needed to get Ricky away from Vegas. Away somewhere safe. Away from the cops.

Angela had one last chance of claiming the man she loved.

***

Abigail poured herself a brandy and looked out the window at the vast sprawl of this desert city.

It had continued to grow and grow.

She remembered coming her as a child with her parents and staying at Treasure Island.

Back in the 80s and the early part of the 90s, Las Vegas was trying to be kid friendly with their themed hotels and fairground rides. Those days were gone now and the city was back to adult themes and large corporate hotels.

The days of $5 shrimp and steak meals and cheap liquor were now a thing of the past. You had to have money to party in Sin City.

A knock on the door broke her train of thought. She unlocked the door and found Cecil standing there. He had been sat outside for extra security.

"Hello, Miss Frost. Dinner is being served in the restaurant. I wondered whether Ricky and you are planning on joining us."

Abigail smiled.

"Ricky is still sleeping. I expect we'll get something later. You go on down though and enjoy it. We'll be safe up here. I'll keep the door locked. Security is still on the desk, I take it?"

"Yes, they are. I'll let them know I'm going to the restaurant and I won't be long," said the big man.

"Please take your time, Cecil. We're fine."

Cecil nodded at Abigail and walked off down the corridor.

She went back to her drink.

Fame and celebrity certainly had their perks, but she often found herself, much like Ricky, spending a lot of time alone in hotel rooms.

The room phone suddenly rang, breaking her trail of thought. She glanced over at Ricky on the bed, but he was sound asleep. He needed this rest. A chance for his brain to slow down and his thoughts to drift away for a while.

He had done amazingly well in his recovery, but Abi knew that, deep down, he still had a way to go. The future was unknown. The only thing she was certain of was that she wanted to spend it with him.

She picked up the phone.

"Hello?"

"Abi, sweetheart, it's Gabriel. How is Ricky? I just heard about what happened earlier. I can't believe it."

"Hello, Gabriel. Ricky was administered a sedative by the doctor and is sleeping. It will do him good."

"Of course. It's the best thing for the poor man," replied Gabriel.

After a moment's silence, he added.

"Look, let me bring up some sandwiches and coffee for you both. I can't have you wasting away now, can I?"

"You really don't need to," said Abigail.

"Nonsense. It will be my pleasure. I'll be ten minutes."

Gabriel hung up the call.

Abigail sat down on the sofa and finished off her drink. She glanced over again at the sleeping figure of Ricky.

He seemed so vulnerable lying there. Yet she knew when he went onto the stage under the spotlight, he became a powerhouse. A rock and roll icon. A true legend. One of a dying breed.

She wondered where the so-called superstars of today's music scene would be in 20 years' time.

Ricky was lucky to have such a loyal team around him. They all seemed so nice and supportive.

This residency had been ideal for him until this latest trouble.

She herself had been used to obsessive fans and the occasional stalker, but these things were usually dealt with swiftly. But if this mad woman was a killer, it made things considerably different.

They didn't see things in a rational manner. They lived in a world created by their own warped logic. They could truly believe that their idol loved them and wanted to be with them. It was scary.

There was a knock on the door and a voice called, "It's me. Gabriel."

Abigail went to the door, opened it and there stood Gabriel with a hostess trolley. She ushered him in as she locked the door.

Gabriel put the trolley by the coffee table.

"We have smoked salmon and cream cheese, prawn mayo and roast beef with horseradish sandwiches, along with chips. Plus, there's water and coffee available."

"You're a star. Thank you," replied Abigail, who suddenly realised that it had been sometime since she had last eaten.

Gabriel glanced over at the bed.

"He looks peaceful."

"He seems to be."

Gabriel walked over to the bed and regarded Ricky closely. A tear came to his eye as he – or rather Angela – thought about all the things that he had done to him.

He reached out and gently stroked his face. Then, a voice in his head brought him back to reality.

Get a grip, you simpering wimp. We have a job to do, so let's do it. And remember, Ricky is mine.

Gabriel moved over to the tray and picked up the coffee pot.

"How do you take it?" he asked Abigail.

"Black, no sugar," she replied.

He poured her a cup and handed it to her.

"Thank you. I could really do with this."

Abigail eagerly took a sip and settled onto the sofa, while Gabriel chose an easychair across from her.

"You're not having a cup?" she asked.

Gabriel smiled.

"I've had my quota of caffeine today, my love. If I have any more, I will be bouncing off the walls."

Abigail smiled, but then her face became serious.

"I'm worried about Ricky. All this recent mayhem again in his life. I'm not sure he can take much more. The news about Max seems to have been the straw that broke the camel's back."

Gabriel leant forward and patted her knee.

"He's a strong character, our Ricky. I promise I'll do everything to help him get through this."

"Do you think the police can catch this mad woman?"

Gabriel regarded Abigail.

"I don't know. She seems to be a step ahead of everybody. She's clever and very devious."

Abigail reached to set her cup on the coffee table, but misjudged her aim. The cup tumbled onto the plush white carpet, leaving an immediate stain.

"Shit!" she exclaimed.

"Are you okay?" asked Gabriel.

Abigail touched her brow. She felt cold sweat there.

"I feel rather strange. Tired, lethargic, dizzy."

Gabriel smiled.

"That will be the ketamine I put in your coffee."

"I don't understand."

Abigail struggled to process what Gabriel had just said, her thoughts muddled. As she reclined back on the sofa, she realised she couldn't move.

Gabriel, aware of the potency of the drug he had given her, knew it would leave her incapacitated for 30 to 45 minutes, erasing all memory of the event.

"Yes. Ketamine. Enough to render you immobile and useless for a while until I decide the best way of disposing of you."

Gabriel approached the trolley and lifted the curtain on the bottom half, revealing the sports bag he had stashed there earlier.

He then made his way to the bathroom.

It was time to prepare for Ricky.

* * *

Ricky jolted awake to a hand shaking his shoulder. As the fog of sleep lifted, he blinked and found himself staring into the face of a redhead.

Was he dreaming again?

He tried to sit up, only to discover that his wrists and ankles were bound by ropes.

"What the fuck? Who are you? What do you want?"

Angela smiled.

"Remember me? I'm your biggest fan, Ricky. You should know that by now. I've adored you for as long as I've known about you. I can't share you with anybody else. It wouldn't be right."

Ricky glanced across the room and saw Abigail slumped motionless on the sofa.

"What have you fucking done to her?"

"Relax Ricky. She's drugged and quite safe for the moment. Her continued wellbeing will be dependent on you."

Ricky regarded Angela.

"What do you want?"

The redhead smiled.

"Simple. I want you, Ricky. You don't need that talentless airhead. You need somebody sophisticated, intelligent and interesting."

"And I suppose that's you?"

"Exactly, sweety. You don't know what you're missing. I worship you, Ricky. I can make you so happy. Dump her and be with me."

Ricky shook his head.

"I love Abi and I will marry her. Make no mistake about that."

Angela stepped back, a flash of anger crossing her face. For a moment, Ricky was struck by a familiar resemblance. Then, he noticed the small tattoo on the inside of her arm, a detail that tugged at the edges of his memory.

He was sure he had seen it recently, but where? His mind felt foggy from the medication he had taken, making it hard to grasp the connection.

"Is that so, Ricky? We'll see about that."

Angela reached into her handbag and produced a wicked looking hunting knife.

"I used a similar knife to dispose of your alcoholic buddy Max. Now I'm going to use it on this whore."

Ricky strained at his bonds, but with no luck.

"For God's sake, I beg you. Don't harm her."

Angela shook her head.

"I have to get rid of her, Ricky. Otherwise, she'll come between you and me."

Ricky roared in anger and disbelief.

"There is no fucking us, you demented bitch. I don't know you. I have millions of fans from all over the world and I respect that, but at the end of the day, they're just fans. They're not part of my private life.

You're not part of it. You never have and you never will be. You are nothing to me. Even if I wanted it, which I don't, how does this whole scenario win me over? You are a sad deluded person who needs help. I don't want you. I will never want you. Give yourself up to the police while you can."

"There is nothing wrong with me," replied Angela.

"Nothing wrong, you say?" answered Ricky, "It's not exactly a sane romantic gesture to have me tied up against my will, drug my fiancée and go on a fucking killing spree. How the fuck would that win my heart? It would tear it out instead. If you kill her, you might as well kill me too."

Angela's face softened and then it looked puzzled as if she couldn't understand why this whole plan hadn't gone the way she intended.

"I did it all for us, Ricky, so we could be together. I don't understand your anger."

She was destined to marry Ricky. She had dreamt about it for years. It was written in the stars. She waited and waited for the opportunity to arise and this was it. Why didn't he feel the same?

"Because I love Abi and you are nothing to me. I repeat, you are fucking nothing. Now cut me lose."

Suddenly, there was a knock on the door and a voice called.

"Boss, are you awake? Miss Frost, are you there?"

It was Cecil.

Before Angela could react, Ricky shouted out.

"Get in here quickly, Cecil."

Angela moved forward and punched Ricky in the face, knocking him back on the bed dazed. She turned towards Abigail, brandishing the knife.

The door imploded inwards, smashed off the hinges. And in lunged Cecil.

He quickly assessed the scene and saw Ricky bleeding from the mouth, tied to the bed, while a redheaded woman advanced toward Abigail Frost with a large knife in her hand.

Cecil charged forward, slamming into Angela and sending her flying across the room to land heavily in the corner. He now picked up the fallen knife, ran to the bed and cut Ricky free.

Ricky swung his legs off the bed, but then recoiled in horror. Standing in the corner of the room was an horrific apparition. The make-up was smeared, blood dripped from the mouth and the red wig was gone.

There stood Gabriel Hart.

The tattoo. Now he remembered. At the hotel pool that morning when he had been swimming.

It had been him all along.

He had cleverly hidden his real identity.

Gabriel moved at speed.

Ricky issued a warning to Cecil.

He turned in time to walk straight into a slicing edge of the hand strike, which connected with his carotid artery. The room began to fade as Cecil dropped the knife on the bed and staggered unsteadily on his feet.

Gabriel moved in for the kill and slapped both of his hands over the big man's eardrums before kneeing him full in the groin. Cecil crumbled to the carpet like a felled oak tree.

Ricky now moved and grabbed for the knife, but Gabriel got there first.

"Gabriel, for pity's sake, stop! What you are doing? I don't understand what the fuck is happening here," cried Ricky.

"I'm not Gabriel. He's gone. I'm Angela."

Angela edged forward, brandishing the blade.

"I don't want to hurt you, Ricky. I love you, but if you don't feel the same…"

Ricky grabbed Angela's wrist with both hands and drove his head into her face. He heard the satisfying crack of bone as the nose broke.

Angela still didn't release the blade and both men struggled for dominance.

Ricky was transformed back to Ruma Island when he fought for his life against Noah and Sydney Rose. He had won then. He had to win again now for Abigail's sake. But this person was fitter, stronger and younger. Ricky's best years were behind him and he was never a fighter anyway.

Angela forced Ricky back onto the bed and straddled his chest. Her face was a mask of blood and hatred. Her eyes were dull and glazed over. They showed no emotion.

"If I can't have you, then nobody can. We will die together here in this room. Then, we'll be together for eternity," she screamed.

Ricky felt his grip weakening and he knew any minute that Angela would free her knife hand.

He now pleaded with Gabriel, praying there was something of the man left there to reason with.

"Gabriel, for Christ's sake. If you're in there, if you can hear me, stop! Don't let her dominate you. Fight back."

For a fleeting second, Gabriel's eyes focused as if seeing Ricky for the first time. Then, they clouded over again.

"You and I must die together now. It's the only way."

Then, out of nowhere, Ricky saw Abigail appear over Gabriel's shoulder. Above her head was a bronze statue of Bacchus that had sat on the bar counter. A very fitting place for the God of wine to reside.

He willed her to strike.

Unsteady on her feet, her head still fuzzy, she summoned the strength to bring the statue down with all her might onto Gabriel's skull.

Gabriel fell away from Ricky and onto the floor.

He didn't move.

Abigail dropped the statue and Ricky embraced her.

"Oh God, Ricky. How terrible."

"Are you okay?" Ricky asked.

"A little groggy, but I'm fine."

She now looked at Ricky's bloodied face.

"What about you?"

Ricky smiled.

"I've had worse."

They embraced again.

Suddenly, an earth-shattering scream split the air and a voice shouted.

"No! He's mine! Die, bitch!"

Angela rose from the floor like a crazed avenging angel and plunged the knife towards Abigail. Ricky stuck his arm out in defence and the blade sliced his right forearm. He hollered out in pain.

As Angela went to stab again, a large powerful arm wrapped around her throat and pulled her clean off her feet.

It was Cecil.

Angela frantically stabbed over her shoulder at the big man, but Cecil kept the hold tight and turned his back stretching Gabriel's spine over his hips. Angela struggled, but it was futile. The strangle was on tight.

"Fuck you, motherfucker. Have a taste of your own medicine, bitch!" yelled Cecil.

Angela became still. The struggling ceased. She was unconscious.

Cecil released her and the body slid to the floor.

Just at that moment, Detective Maria Cortez appeared in the doorway with her gun drawn. Not far behind her was security man, Cody Wilson, gun also in hand, followed by another police officer.

They surveyed the room and the carnage.

Ricky and Abigail were on the bed. Abigail had wrapped a pillowcase around Ricky's wounded arm, but the blood was still seeping through.

Cecil was leant back against the wall breathing heavily covered in a sheen of sweat.

What appeared to be the body of Gabriel Hart dressed in a green Ralph Lauren dress and Christian Louboutin heels was lying on the carpet.

Cortez looked at everybody.

"Okay, guys. What the hell went on here?"

Chapter 20

Everyone sat in the Chameleon Lounge, nursing drinks from the bar – everyone except Detective Cortez and Ricky.

Gabriel Hart, now Angela, had regained consciousness and was promptly arrested, cuffed and taken to the police station.

The scene of the incident had been thoroughly examined.

Detective Cortez had taken the statements of Ricky, Abigail and Cecil.

She had earlier gone to the address given to her by Detective Norton and had found his body there. On checking it, she found a weak pulse and immediately phoned for the paramedics.

Cortez hurried back to the hotel after the officer she had left there informed her that Gabriel's car had returned and was parked in its space.

A recent update told her that Norton was alive and recovering.

His neck was severely bruised. The delicate hyoid bone was still intact and there would be no lasting damage to the windpipe. He had been extremely fortunate.

Being a bear of a man, his strong neck muscles had helped him survive the savage chokehold.

The apartment at the Oasis, which Gabriel had rented, was thoroughly searched.

Inside, it resembled a shrine to Ricky Wilder, with photos and newspaper clippings covering the walls, along with memorabilia, including Ricky's missing vest top. Dozens of scrapbooks were found, filled with clippings dating back to the early Stormtrooper days and continuing through the Ruma murders and their aftermath. Recent photos of the inside of the murder house on Ruma Island, *An Diadan*, were also discovered, along with images of Ricky here in Las Vegas.

The wardrobe was full of hundreds of dollars of women's dresswear, shoes, wigs and make-up. Gabriel had lived a dual identity for some time, successfully keeping the two sides of his life separate and hidden from most people. Sometimes he was Gabriel, other times Angela, and occasionally aware that he was both.

In the weeks that followed, Gabriel/Angela was interviewed numerous times, and it was determined that 'they' were responsible for the deaths of Max Sinclair outside Queenie's and Edward Bryson in the restroom of the Harley Davidson bar, as well as the attempted murders of Detective Ernest Norton, Ricky Wilder, and Abigail Frost.

It was also disclosed that 'they' had murdered security guard Jack Myers. Gabriel thought the old man would recall that he saw him deliver the card and rose to Ricky's room and he couldn't risk that, so he had visited his apartment and pushed him down the stairs.

"Well, everybody. I think this wraps up the case of the mystery redhead. Ironically, the murderer was among you all the time."

"I can't believe it was Gabriel. He was a friend to us all," said Joey Bruce.

"It's hard to comprehend, but it was Angela who did most of the killing, not Gabriel. But she also coerced him into doing her dirty work. In the end, she became so dominant he couldn't fight her. They really were two separate people in one body. Like brother and sister," answered Cortez.

"That is some fucked up shit," replied Cecil.

Ricky sipped on a mineral water, still on painkillers due to the knife wound that had required 20 stitches. Thankfully, it hadn't severed any nerves or tendons, so once healed, he would still be able to play his beloved guitar.

The medical staff had wanted to keep him in hospital overnight for checks, but he had refused. He wanted to get back to Abigail who had recovered from the effects of the ketamine.

Putting his glass down, he said, "It fucks with my mind, but he really was two separate people."

Cortez nodded.

"That's right. Early indications suggest he was a paranoid schizophrenic or suffered from dissociative identity disorder."

"What the fuck is that?" asked Cecil.

Cortez regarded the big man.

"As I understand it – although I'm no expert – if you have dissociative identity disorder, you will experience intense changes in your identity. You may feel like different aspects of your identity are in control of your behaviour and thoughts at different times. This can happen in various ways. When the urge to become Angela got too strong, this is who Gabriel became.

Sometimes he would have no knowledge of what he did or where he went. The female personality just took over. In the end, I guess the battle to control the personalities became out of control and Angela won."

The room was silent for a moment as everybody present mulled over what they had been told.

"Did he have any living family?" asked Abigail.

"Not that we're aware of. We will, of course, be looking into his background in the coming days."

"The poor bastard," said Ricky, "How the fuck do people like that go undetected and just walk around in society as they please?"

"That is a big question to ask, which I don't have the answer for. I just catch criminals," answered Cortez.

"The authorities are to blame. The system is fucked. These people should be looked after," said Janice Strickland.

"Maybe he was just born with that bad gene in him," mused Joey Bruce.

"We'll never know for sure," replied Cortez.

"Anyway, I must head back to the precinct. I'll be in touch with any further developments. Will you carry on with the residency, Ricky?"

Ricky raised his arm.

"The medics reckon a month for this to heal and then I'll be back. I can't let the fans down now, can I?"

Everybody laughed at the sardonic comment.

Chapter 21

When everybody else had gone to bed, Ricky and Abigail sat quietly together in the Chameleon Lounge.

Ricky ran the last week back in his mind. He could now see clues everywhere.

Gabriel, in his position of authority and trust at the Sunset, was able to move around the hotel in plain sight without arousing any suspicion.

When Angela's dominant personality grew stronger, she compelled Gabriel to act, like delivering the rose and the card.

Ultimately, Gabriel lost any control he had over her, and Angela's obsessive and dangerous persona took over completely.

She convinced herself that she was the love of Ricky's life and could not tolerate anyone else being near him. In her delusion, she believed Ricky loved her in return. Her obsession with him had completely distorted her grasp on reality.

"I thought I was going to lose you," Ricky said.

Abigail smiled sadly.

"And I you."

Ricky softly kissed her.

She looked into his eyes.

"I feel sorry for Gabriel. What a terrible way to live your life."

Ricky nodded.

"I can hardly believe this has all happened."

"Will you be okay, Ricky? God knows Ruma Island was bad enough, but this... this might be enough to push you over the edge."

Ricky saw the concern in her face.

"I will have to take one day at a time, but as long as you're with me, I'll be fine."

She laid her head on his shoulder and they both sat quietly with their thoughts.

Ricky continued.

"I've been rethinking my situation, and after the next residency, I'm going to retire. We'll find a quiet, isolated place to call home, so when you finish your work, you'll have a haven to return to. How does that sound?"

"Idyllic, Ricky, but please don't rush into anything."

"Abi, this residency and the impending album has been beyond my wildest dreams. It's my swansong. I've been fortunate not only in my career but in my life," replied Ricky.

Abi laughed.

"Some people might beg to differ with you, my love."

"I am alive, Abi. I've survived again, but like a cat, I'm running out of lives. I got lucky. No, it's time for Ricky Wilder to fade into the background and into rock folklore. I've spent a lifetime in the public eye. It's time to step out of it and enjoy what life I have left. If you wish to spend it with me, then I'll be the happiest man alive."

Abigail hugged Ricky.

"I'm with you all the way."

Epilogue

Six months later

Ricky stepped out the back door of his farmhouse into the crisp autumn morning. Sipping from his coffee mug, he admired the majestic mountains beyond his expansive garden. The watery sun hung high in the sky as he inhaled the fragrant scents of pine and heather.

Suddenly, he felt an arm wrap around his waist and turned to see Abi – or rather, Mrs. Wilder.

He kissed her and smelt her hair, fresh and clean from the shower.

As promised, he completed his final residency and announced his retirement just a few days after he and Abi returned to the UK. They were married shortly afterwards in a small church in Berkshire, with only a handful of close friends in attendance.

It was a low-key affair and *Hello* magazine or the media were not told about it or invited.

Ricky sold his house in Berkshire and his apartment in LA.

His new home now was a secret bolthole in the Highlands of Scotland well away from the prying eyes of fans and paparazzi.

Ricky bought an 100-year-old stone farmhouse and 20 acres of land, which included stables and its own lake complete with trout.

His life now was a complete turnaround from the music business.

* * *

Abi travelled between the States and the UK with her work. She still had her apartment in LA. The seventh season of *New York Blue* was in the pipeline as it went from success to success on Netflix.

She was gaining more and more fame in the acting world and had just signed up to co-star in a movie with Bradley Cooper. Her star was shining brightly.

She was becoming hot property after many years of walk-on and bit parts.

She had just wrapped up appearances on the *Graham Norton Show* and *Lorraine* here in the UK, as well as *The View*, America's most-watched daytime chat show.

Success was coming thick and fast, but she had her rock, Ricky, to keep her grounded. After all, he had been there and done it all before.

These days, he was more relaxed and at home here in the Highlands. He didn't seem to miss the music scene.

He had taken up fishing, golf and hiking. He also liked to wild swim in the many lochs in and around the area.

His arm had healed well from the knife wound, leaving a scar that joined the bullet wound scar and the remnant of a missing ear. He often mused that a war veteran who had done a few tours might come back home with fewer scars. After all, he had only been a rock star.

He still enjoyed playing his guitar, but only for himself and Abigail.

Ricky continued to experience the nightmares of Ruma and now Angela had been added to them. Ironically, on Ruma, Sidney had wanted to kill him because she hated him and in Las Vegas, Angela had wanted to kill him because she loved him. How fucked up was that.

He had grown to live with the bad dreams.

Joey Bruce still kept in touch and had tried to persuade Ricky to come to Japan to do a series of acoustic gigs, following the number one success of his album, but he turned it down flat. In the end, even Joey realised that he was deadly serious about his retirement.

The press and media had wanted interviews about the whole Las Vegas incident, but this time, Ricky refused. He did one exclusive interview in the UK and one in the USA, and that was it.

He had enough of the circus. Plus, he had really liked Gabriel and felt deep sorrow for him. He wasn't going to exploit him for monetary gain.

In the aftermath of the incident, a renowned Swedish psychiatrist, Sven Andersson, studied the case of Gabriel Hart. After interviewing him for the police, he concluded that Gabriel had suffered from dissociative identity disorder, or DID. During these interviews, Gabriel/Angela confessed to two murders that had gone undetected in their earlier years

People with DID have two or more distinct personalities that are not merely shifts in traits or moods. Instead, a person with DID exhibits significant differences between these alternate identities.

Often, these personalities are completely different from one another, with each fragmented identity taking control of the person's identity for a time.

The individual maintains a primary or host identity, which is their original self, and responds to their given name. This primary identity is generally a more passive, trusted source and may be unaware of the other personalities.

When a personality change occurs, the new identity has its own distinct history, behaviours and characteristics. These split personalities, or alters, often possess their own names, ages, genders, moods, memories and vocabulary.

A new personality often perceives themselves differently; for instance, someone assigned male at birth may have an alternate identity as a woman and experience themselves with female biological characteristics. The shift between these personalities typically occurs in response to specific stressors or triggers.

The exact cause of DID is not fully understood, but there is a strong link between the condition and trauma. This connection is particularly evident in cases of trauma or abuse during childhood, though it may also stem from factors present from birth.

A person with DID may live with their dual personalities in harmony, or one may become more dominant and potentially destructive. When these alternate identities take over, they often exhibit different vocabulary and gestures. In some cases, one personality might adopt habits that the other does not, such as smoking or exhibiting violent behaviour.

During the shift from one personality to another, individuals may experience various symptoms. Some may feel anxious about the personality change, while others could become very angry or even violent. Some individuals may not notice or remember these transitions, although those around them might.

Specific personalities may emerge in response to particular situations, and these symptoms can cause significant distress, disrupting a person's ability to live normally. Additional symptoms may include amnesia, a distorted sense of time, trance-like states, out-of-body experiences, engaging in behaviours that are atypical for the individual and sleep disturbances.

A person with DID may also experience symptoms of other conditions, including self-harm. One study indicates that more than 70% of individuals with DID have attempted suicide, while two other studies found that 17% of people with DID committed homicide.

Gabriel had been a deeply troubled and confused individual.

In today's world, many people shout about mental health issues over trivial matters, seeking attention. But for Gabriel, it had been a real living hell.

Gabriel/Angela had harboured an unhealthy fascination for Ricky Wilder. One that went far beyond normal fan worship.

Angela truly believed that she was the love of Ricky's life and when he had come to the Sunset Hotel, where her alter ego Gabriel worked, she saw it as a sign for her to reveal herself and declare her undying love for him.

Things hadn't gone the way she planned.

Nobody would fully understand what had happened to Gabriel Hart. They could only speculate or lend their professional opinion.

Gabriel David Hart is still undergoing psychiatric tests to determine his sentence and incarceration.

Nevada State still has the death penalty by lethal injection.

Time will tell the outcome.

Now all Ricky wanted to do was forget everything and enjoy his days with Abi.

Every sunrise was a blessing.

When he had been at the height of his career, one day melted into the next and he had taken everything for granted. Not now though.

"I thought, since I have to go back to the States on Monday, we might take a drive down to the local village for a pub lunch and then stop by the local store to pick up something nice for dinner tonight. What do you think?" said Abi.

"Sounds perfect. I'll go get my coat and the car keys," answered Ricky.

As Ricky headed to the kitchen, he heard a knock on the front door. It must be the postman, he thought, as they rarely got visitors in such a remote area.

He walked to the hall and opened the front door, only to find nobody there. Peering down the drive, he saw no post van or anyone else in sight.

Strange. Maybe he had imagined it.

Then he noticed it, and a chill of fear ran down his spine.

On the doorstep lay a single red rose...

About the Author

Kevin O'Hagan lives just outside Bristol with his wife. He has three grown-up children and five grandchildren.

Kevin has had a passion for writing since he was a child but has no formal writing training. Everything he has learnt has been a personal voyage of discovery.

One of his favourite sayings is, "If you want to get better at writing, then write."

Starstruck is his 11th work of fiction to date.

Kevin is a semi-retired world-renowned martial artist. He holds an 8th Dan black belt in Jujutsu after more than 49 years of training and teaching. These days, he still teaches part-time.

His hobbies are reading, writing, playing guitar, going to the gym and travelling.

www.kevinohagan.com for more information.

Other Books by the Author

If you enjoyed this book, then check
out other stories by Kevin.
Read a little about them on the following pages.
Available at Amazon, Waterstones and all good
bookstores.

For more information, visit www.kevinohagan.com
or join the group "Kevin O'Hagan
Author's Corner" on Facebook.

Coming in 2025...

THE CUPBOARD OF BAD DREAMS

Bite size stories with a killer twist

by
Kevin O'Hagan

Read a little now on the next page...

Ambush

Joe Kramer drove his Jaguar F-PACE as fast as possible along the dark country roads. He had to hold back speed on the big 2.0-litre 4-cylinder engine on these unfamiliar lanes. Luckily, traffic was non-existent in this remote area, especially as it was past midnight. He was in a hurry. His mind was reeling from the events of earlier that evening. It should never have come to this, but he was left with no choice. Now he had to sort things out and put together a plan.

His thoughts were interrupted when his headlights picked up the shape of a vehicle pulled up on a grass verge ahead. It was parked rather precariously, with its back end jutted out onto the road. It looked like somebody had parked it up in a hurry.

He slowed his car because it was going to be a tight squeeze through the gap it had left. "What a prick to go parking there," thought Kramer as he carefully manoeuvred his Jaguar around it.

He noticed that the other vehicle was a grey Land Rover. The passenger door was open, and the interior light shone. Kramer glanced in the driver's side window as he passed. It was empty. Strange.

He picked up speed once more and soon saw the Land Rover disappear from view as he rounded a bend in the road. Then, to his amazement, a semi-naked girl ran out of the surrounding woodland in front of his car waving her arms frantically. Kramer had to jam on the brakes to avoid knocking her down.

He cursed loudly as he got the car under control and brought it to a jolting stop. He quickly glanced in the back seat and then out of the windscreen. The girl was approaching the car. She looked frightened. She was clad only in her bra and panties. He also noticed that her body was streaked with dirt and blood. The girl ran around to the driver's side window as Joe lowered it down.

"Help me, please. Quick! You must help! He tried to kill me… my sister is still in the woods with him. Please come."

Kramer tried to slow the girl's babbling down.

"Okay, calm down. You're safe now. What happened?"

"We were hitchhiking earlier. He picked us up. He seemed so nice and then he changed…"

The girl became hysterical again.

"You have got to come now. There's no time to waste. He's still got my sister. He was raping her. I escaped. She may be dead. Please come!"

Kramer gritted his teeth. Christ, this was all he needed right now. He was in a hurry himself. No time to lose.

He glanced back to the car's rear seat once more to see his eight-month-old son Ben still sound asleep in his car seat. He turned back to the girl and looked at her pleading eyes.

"Did you ring the police?" Kramer asked.

"No, he took our phones."

Part of him wanted to drive off, but somehow, he couldn't bring himself to leave the girl. He made his decision. The police weren't coming, so he was this girl's only hope.

"Is this man armed?"

The girl nodded.

"He has a gun and a large hunting knife."

Kramer jumped out of the car, locked it, stole one more glance at his son and then set off with the girl.

"Wait a second," he said.

He went to the boot of his car, opened it and produced a baseball bat. He then followed the disappearing figure of the girl.

Kramer caught up with her as they crashed through the undergrowth.

"What's your name?"

The girl spoke as she ran on.

"My name is Sarah and my sister is Becky. As I said, we were hitchhiking when this guy picked us up. He seemed okay. But he turned out to be a pervert. He stopped by these woods and forced us by gun point to follow him and then he attacked us. He just went crazy."

Kramer took all this in and nodded.

"How much further is it?"

"Not far now," replied Sarah, "I just hope to God that Becky's alright."

Finally, they approached a small clearing and Kramer came to a halt and surveyed the scene. He saw another girl, naked curled up in a ball by a tree. Blood and dirt also streaked her body. Next to her lay the body of a middle-aged man. He had a large hunting knife embedded in his white flabby stomach.

"Jesus Christ, what the fuck has happened here?!" exclaimed Kramer...

Battlescars

Tony Slade Novel number 1

Some wounds run deep. Can they ever heal?

Tony Slade sits in a coffee shop waiting. He is reflecting on his dark and violent past. He is waiting for the woman he loves, but he is also waiting for the man who wants him dead. Who will reach him first? The clock is ticking...

Tony Slade is used to dealing with violence and death. He has made a career out of it. From boxer to bouncer, paratrooper, and mercenary to minder. But now, he is getting older and he wants out. He has miraculously found love and he has one last chance at happiness, but it will come with a price. The woman he loves is not his; she belongs to a very dangerous man. A man who you don't want to cross. But Tony is ready to risk it all on one last roll of the dice before a powder keg of violence explodes.

But that is not all. Unknown to him, there is another threat coming his way. One that he will not see until the last moment. Who will get out alive?

Tough times call for tough people. Tony Slade is one such person.

No Hiding Place
Tony Slade Novel number 2

You can run but you can't hide forever.

They say time is a great healer. But for Tony Slade time is running out. The physical scars are healing, but the mental ones are still raw. Waking up in hospital after the coffee shop massacre and finding he has cheated death; he needs to know why. But he has now become a man everybody wants to question. All he wants to do is disappear forever, but some people will not let that happen.

Suddenly, Tony is hounded by the press and media. He is also trailed by the tenacious DCI Wyatt and hunted by a psychotic killer who is relentless, and hell bent on revenge.

Tony Slade is in hiding recovering from the bullet wounds and the trauma of recent events that have changed his life forever. Hiding on the tiny, isolated island of *Graig O Mor* in the Bristol Channel, Tony knows that it is only a matter of time until he is found. Then, he will have to stop running and make a stand against an enemy who will not give up. It will become a matter of life and death.

*A storm is coming from the mainland
to the Island of Graig O Mor.*

Last Stand

Tony Slade Novel number 3

Blood is thicker than water

Tony Slade is living in the Canary Islands. He is resting and soaking up the sun. He is keeping his head down under an assumed identity and trying to forget the last few traumatic years where he has experienced love, violence, heartbreak and death.

Tony is a survivor. An ex-paratrooper and mercenary who has seen more than his fair share of action, but those days are well behind him now. Or so he thought.

He is no longer a young man and the fire that used to burn like an inferno in his belly is now just flickering. Tony is looking for a quiet life into retirement when he receives a shocking and lifechanging piece of news. A secret that has been buried for years has suddenly came to light.

This secret will force Tony out of hiding to return to the UK and back into the violent world of gangsters, drugs and crime.

Pursued all the time by an old nemesis, Tony must pull all his fighting skills together to face a dangerous and deadly drug lord who has something of his that he wants back at any cost. Tony knows that blood will spill in one final stand.

This time, it's personal

Killing Time

Joe Regan Novel 1

Ex-Scotland Yard policeman DCI Joe Regan had retired from the force after a particularly vicious attempt on his life, which had him on the critical list in hospital, but his gritty Gaelic spirit and resolve helped him recover.

Now leading a new life running an antiques emporium in the sleepy town of Oakcombe in the West Country, he is trying to put his past behind him. But unknown to Joe, a burglary at the nearby country home of famous TV celebrity Ron Goodwin opens up a nasty can of worms in the form of something hidden within an antique clock which finds its way to his shop.

This something could ruin Ron Goodwin's career just as he is about to crack America. The dark secrets contained within the clock cannot afford to fall into the wrong hands, so it must be found at all costs, even if it means murder.

Joe Regan suddenly finds himself embroiled in a race to find the clock and its contents as they go missing, before a hired killer who will stop at nothing does. But when Joe inadvertently stumbles across the secret, he now becomes the next target.

The clock is ticking, and time is running out.

A Change of Heart

*Can a heart transplant victim inherit
the characteristics of their donor?*

Simon Winter is a prime candidate for a heart attack. Middle aged, sedentary and grossly overweight. His lifestyle is driving him to an early grave, but he is ignoring all the signs until it is too late.

He has a failed marriage behind him, a boring job and a fear of violence and blood. He has lived a safe and uneventful life, avoiding confrontation and danger until now where this is all about to change dramatically.

Eddie Prince is an ex-professional boxer and minor television celebrity. He has had a turbulent life out of the ring, which has resulted in prison time. Money has come and gone as he has a gambling addiction, which results in him owing a lot of money to some bad people. He has run away to what he hopes is a better life, but his old life is about to catch up with him, resulting in dire circumstances.

These two men are about to connect in a way they could never have dreamed of. Two men at different ends of the spectrum. Two men who are chalk and cheese. Two men who have nothing in common until one inherits the other's heart after a transplant.

Now one will use the other as a vessel of revenge to find the man who murdered him and settle a score with shocking conclusions.

Blood Tracks

At one time in the 1980s, Stormtrooper were the most successful rock band on the planet. Everything they touched turned to gold. But among all the fame was jealousy and greed. This resulted in the sacking of their iconic lead singer Jimmy Parrish for drug usage, which endangered the band's continued success.

Sometime later after a bitter break-up, Jimmy Parrish apparently committed suicide in mysterious circumstances. His body was never found. A proposed warts and all book on the band that he had been approached to write would now never happen, a blessing for some.

The Mark 2 line-up of the band went on to have global success and entered the Rock and Roll Hall of Fame as one of the biggest rock bands of all time. Even when they finally split up, the spectre of Jimmy Parrish never fully went away.

Fast forward twenty years, the band have reformed to record a new album. They are heading for the remote island of Ruma off the Outer Hebrides. Ruma is a wild isolated place of mystery and intrigue. They will stay at the grand house of a reclusive film director who has a state-of-the-art recording studio in the bowels of the building.

Storm Alec is due to hit the island. It will cut it and its inhabitants off from the rest of civilisation. But worse is to come as a mysterious killer lurks within the walls of the house hellbent on murdering each and every member of the band and their recording crew.

Who is it and what is their motive?

There is nowhere to run and nowhere to hide. Nobody is coming to help.

As the body count rises, who - if anybody - can survive.

Making a hit record can sometimes be murder.

The Key to Murder

Is money the root of all evil?

Imagine that you found a key. A key that opened a locker. A locker that contained a holdall. A holdall that contained money. A lot of money. £350,000 to be exact in used untraceable notes.

What would you do?

Put it back in the locker and walk away? Contact the police? Or take it?

It is a life changing sum.

But what if that money belonged to a dangerous man? A man who will stop at nothing to get it back. He will relentlessly track you down and anybody who gets in his way will suffer.

This is what happens when the worlds of three men clash.

Ronnie Moon, Tommy Scott and Adam Lucas are all involved in a deadly game of Cat and Mouse. Each want the money for different reasons.

The hunt is on, but who will survive?

Their greed and ambition could just be the Key to Murder.

If you want to know what man is really like, take notice of what he is really like when he loses money.

Murder in Store

"You know what they say about curiosity, don't you?"

Chris Cooper is nicknamed the 'Nighthawk'. He and his friends are urban explorers. They love to enter abandoned buildings and structures and search them, especially at night when nobody else is around. The activity is illegal, but it gives them such a buzz that it becomes addictive. They love to flirt with danger.

Eddie Creed is on the run to Bristol. He has inadvertently crossed 'Big Baz' Watkins, a London criminal with a nasty reputation. Eddie only wanted to help the girl, but now his world is turned upside down as three hitmen are on his trail. Their agenda is to kill him.

On this particular cold winter's evening, Chris and his friends will enter and explore the empty store of the iconic Radley's in Bristol city centre.

On this same night. Eddie Creed, who is being chased down by the hitmen, seeks refuge and finds it in the same store. When the killers also enter the store and block off its only exit, a shocking and horrifying series of events begins to unfold.

Suddenly, the worlds of Eddie Creed and Chris Cooper and his friends collide as mayhem and murder occurs. Now, they are all running for their lives as they are relentlessly hunted down.

There will be murder in store!

Buried Secrets

Joe Regan Novel 2

What if an enduring legend proved to be true? A legend that most people dismissed in the same way as Sasquatch, the Loch Ness Monster, Excalibur and the Tooth Fairy?

What if this legend spoke of priceless religious artefacts buried and hidden by Celtic monks from the invading barbarian hordes sailing to the British Isles? Treasures so cleverly hidden that they have lay undiscovered for centuries, waiting to be found.

Professor Declan Byrne of Trinity College Dublin thinks that he has evidence to the whereabouts of such treasures. Evidence that he has outlined in a journal.

If true, it will be the find of the century.

But somebody else has found this out and wants the journal at any costs. They will stop at nothing to get their hands on it. Even murder. And so, the hunt to find the treasure begins. Desperate measures will be taken to be the first person to find it.

Joe Regan, former DCI in the Metropolitan Police and now antiques dealer, is holidaying on the south coast of Ireland with his girlfriend Maggie. He is retracing his family's heritage and reliving a few memories from his childhood there.

He had not planned on being suddenly caught up in a web of mystery and crime concerning Celtic treasures, drug smuggling and murder. But it seems trouble follows Joe wherever he goes, and he is going to have to all his resources and experience to keep himself one step ahead of the hunt and, more importantly, stay alive.

Avenging Angel

Never mistake law for justice

It's nearly Christmas and the streets of Bristol have a killer on them. The police have no clues as to who this person may be. The media have coined them 'The Ghost'. They take their victim's life with military-like precision and then seemingly disappear into the night.

DCI Harry Bowe and his team are up against it as they need to get a break in the case and attain the killer's identity fast. The powers above are breathing down their neck.

The problem for Bowe is that all the killings have been of criminals. But nothing links these people, except the fact that they were lowlifes who flaunted the law and thought they were above it.

Until now.

The bottom line is a vigilante has taken the law into their own hands and the press and media are getting ready for a field day.

As the murders increase, so does the pressure on DCI Bowe to deliver.

But it's not only the police who want to catch this killer. Charlie Rawlings, a local gangster, can't have random murders on his patch. He has an important deal coming down and the last thing he needs is a crazed killer spoiling things, so he decides to do what the police are failing to do and find this person for himself.

But in Rawling's case, when he finds them, he will kill them.

But not only is this killer elusive; they're also extremely dangerous and determined to carry on their campaign of murder.

They will not be stopped.

Beware!
Michael the Archangel is out there in the
shadows and ready to claim your soul.

A Final Word from the Author

When you have finished this book or any of my previous ones, please can you leave a review online. It really does help and will only take a few minutes of your time.

I would love to read your feedback.

Many thanks,

Kevin

www.ingramcontent.com/pod-product-compliance
Ingram Content Group UK Ltd.
Pitfield, Milton Keynes, MK11 3LW, UK
UKHW041949110325
456116UK00001B/4